THE

MAGNIFICENT
12

BOOK FOUR

THE POWER

**Other Magnificent 12 books
by Michael Grant**

The Magnificent 12: The Call
The Magnificent 12: The Trap
The Magnificent 12: The Key

MICHAEL GRANT

THE MAGNIFICENT 12

BOOK FOUR

THE POWER

HarperCollins *Children's Books*

First published in the USA by HarperCollins *Publishers* Inc in 2013

First published in Great Britain by HarperCollins *Children's Books* in 2013

HarperCollins *Children's Books* is a division of HarperCollins*Publishers* Ltd,
77-85 Fulham Palace Road, Hammersmith, London W6 8JB

www.harpercollins.co.uk

1

978-0-00-739596-5

Printed and bound in England by Clays Ltd, St Ives plc.

For Katherine, Jake, and Julia

Not Far from the Earth's Molten Core (Present Day)

Princess Ereskigal, whose friends (she had no friends) all called her Risky, was having a very difficult conversation with her mother, the Pale Queen.

"Are they destroyed?" the Pale Queen nagged. "Are the new Magnificent Twelve all dead?"

The Pale Queen could appear in just about any form she chose, but for the purposes of this particular conversation she was wearing one of her favorite forms: as tall as a moderate redwood tree, with a gigantic head—a quite beautiful head in some ways, but with skin so translucent that in the right light you could see the bones of her skull and her jaw and the individual teeth in her head, thirty-six of them in all, each long and sharp and curved back to facilitate the swallowing of large, whole, usually living things.

Her hair was white. Actually it was colorless if you looked at an individual strand, but taken all together it was white (like a polar bear's). It went down to her bony shoulders, from which hung a floor-length robe made out of screams.

Not the sort of outfit you find for sale at your local mall. But the Pale Queen wove reality out of fear and loss and despair.[1]

The dress had a cutaway so that you could see her powerful calves filling boots as tall as city light posts. The boots were dragon skin and used human skulls to make a row of buckles. The toes of the boots were about as big as canoes—sharp, barbed-steel canoes.

Frankly, Risky thought, the outfit was a bit "young" for her mother. But she wasn't going to say anything about it unless her mother really annoyed her. She was

---

1 She was not a nice person.

holding that in reserve.

"Mother, I said I would do it, didn't I?" Risky huffed.

"So, the new Magnificent Twelve have been destroyed?"

"Are you saying you don't trust me?" Risky crossed her arms over her chest and actually stamped her foot.

Like the Pale Queen, Risky could take any form. But generally she preferred to appear as an extraordinarily attractive teenage girl with luscious red hair and eyes so green there was no way they could possibly be entirely human.

Her dress was a simple, formfitting thing with a neckline that was daring without being "too much." And she most often went barefoot.

"I trust . . . NO ONE!" the Pale Queen raged. And when she raged, her minions—Skirrit, Tong Elves, Gudridan, Lepercons, and so on—were blown back like action figures in the blast of a leaf blower.

Risky wasn't blown anywhere.

She feared her mother, as any sensible daughter would. There wasn't a lot of motherly love in this family, and the Pale Queen could absolutely decide to gobble her daughter up like a shrimp. Which was exactly what she had done to Risky's father.

Like a shrimp.

But at the same time, the Pale Queen needed Risky. For another few days the Pale Queen was bound by a powerful spell and could not escape the World Beneath and go romping around up top where all the tasty humans lived.

Risky, however, could.

Which meant Risky could take on jobs like eliminating the terrible threat posed by the Magnificent Twelve. A task she had so far failed to accomplish despite several attempts.

"I don't think you're taking this seriously," the Pale Queen said more quietly, her tone larded with guilt-inducing disappointment.

"I am so," Risky countered.

"No, you're not."

"Uh-huh!"

"No."

"Yah-ha-ah!"

"I just don't want you being distracted. Remember the last time?"

That was unfair.

That was a cheap shot.

A low blow.

Because yes, Risky did remember the last time she'd made a promise to her mother, a thousand years ago. . . .

. . . And as you can see by the ellipses, the three little dots there, we're going to tell that story. Later. But first, on to chapter 1.

One

It turned out the Punjab was in India. Did you know that? No, you didn't; don't pretend. But don't feel bad, either, because David "Mack" MacAvoy also had no idea where the Punjab was until very recently. He's learned a lot about the Punjab lately.

For instance, he learned that the Punjab[2] is a warm, sunny place, at least at this particular time of year. Mack noticed how sunny and warm it was because he

---

2 Why do they call it "the" Punjab rather than just Punjab? There's a perfectly good explanation, but it wouldn't fit in a footnote. Also, there's some more Punjab in Pakistan, but let's stick with India. One Punjab is plenty.

was on the ground staring right up at that warm sunny sun.

He was on the ground because creatures called Brembles were keeping him there.

Do you know what a Bremble is? Probably not, because Brembles no longer exist. (The last Bremble died in 1797, and he was quite old by then.) Brembles were a hybrid species, not something that occurred naturally, but a species created by evil forces. Imagine a large gorilla. No, twice that big. Now imagine that instead of being a peaceable plant eater, that oversized gorilla was extremely unpleasant. Now imagine that instead of fur, that extremely unpleasant oversized gorilla was covered in something very like porcupine quills. So, already: not good.

But now imagine that the porcupine quills were the least of it, because where a gorilla would have hands, Brembles had what looked like some terrible explosion of thorns, spikes, and razor wire. From the center of this melee of thorns, spikes, and razor wire protruded one spike, longer than the others, which was known as a chulk. This chulk was split so that it was really two spikes with a narrow gap between them, rather like two tines of a fork.

It was these chulks that the Brembles used to pin Mack in place. They had driven their chulks deep into the ground in such a way as to pin his four limbs down.

In addition to being staked out, he was also stretched a bit so that the muscles in his chest felt almost as if they might tear. This made it hard to breathe, which in turn made it hard to scream, which was okay because there was no one to come to his rescue.

Did he want to scream? Definitely.

Mack was utterly unable to reach a hand to his face, which was a shame because there were red ants crawling into his ears and nose and scouting around his eyeballs. These were not the little ants you might see at a picnic. These ants were not trying to get at the coleslaw. Unless *coleslaw* is a euphemism for *Mack's brain*.

Mack had a pretty good view of one ant in particular that was walking right across his eyeball—his left eyeball, as it happened. Mack blinked furiously, hoping to discourage the ant, but each sweep of his eyelid just knocked the ant around a little, which is no way to discourage an ant.

Seen in extreme close-up, the ant was like some fuzzy, out-of-focus, terrifying alien robot. It had six legs, a carapace,[3] and a rounded-off pyramid of a head with huge, elongated pincers on the front. It had little black BBs for eyes. And its tail had a stinger like a combination claw and shot needle that would squirt painful venom if stabbed into something.

Like, say, an eyeball.

In all honesty, the ants were not as creepy as the giraffe-necked beetles that had been exploring Mack's face just minutes before. But Mack had gotten rid of the beetles using his *enlightened puissance*—the mystical power possessed by only a few—and some words from the Vargran language—known to even fewer.

All he'd had to do was yell, "*Lom-ma fabfor!*"[4] and the beetles had disappeared. Mack had been studying his Vargran. He was all Vargraned up. He had come to the Punjab ready for trouble. Just one little problem: the *enlightened puissance* isn't some endless water faucet with power just flowing out like, well, water. No, it's more like a *drip drip drip* of water. It comes, then it

---

3 Nope. No idea what a carapace is.
4 "Disappear, beetles!"

stops, then slowly, sloooowly it builds back up until there's enough to drip. A treasonous Tong Elf had once told him it took a full day, but Tong Elves lied. Still, it took a while, and while you were waiting for it to build back up . . . you'd find that ants had replaced the beetles, and now where were you?

Well, you were staked out by the chulks of Brembles in the Punjab with ants in your eyeballs, that's where you were.

"Ahhhh!" he gasped because right then an ant bit him. Not the eyeball ant. An ear ant. An ant just inside his ear. The bottom part of the ear canal, if you want to be really specific.

It felt exactly like someone had heated a needle over a fire and then stabbed it into his ear canal. Not good.

"Ahhhh!" Mack cried again, straining for breath. "That hurts!"

"Aha! I see they are biting," Valin gloated. "That's very bad news, Mack, my timeless foe, because once one ant starts, they all get into it. Within a minute, a hundred ants will sink their painful stingers into you! You will cry out in pain. Then you will swell up. And of course die. And thus will my family's honor be avenged!"

"I am not your timeless foe, you lunatic!"

Valin was standing over him but providing no shade from the blazing sun above. He was dressed flamboyantly in puffy zebra-striped pantaloons, black leather boots that rose to his knees, and a purple vest over no shirt. To top it all off, he had an amazing hat that looked like the kind of thing Puss in Boots or maybe a pirate might wear. It had an actual pink feather. From his wide belt hung a dagger and a short sword.

It was an eccentric look.

Beyond Valin stood the terrible Nafia[5] assassin Paddy "Nine Iron" Trout. Paddy was an elderly gentleman dressed all in green. Green suede shoes, green slacks, a green-and-yellow waistcoat over a very pale green shirt but beneath a bright-green sport coat. And on top of his shiny, bald head, there was a green bowler hat.

Even in India, which is a diverse and tolerant country known for interesting clothing, Valin and Paddy stood out. It's not every day you see a pantalooned twelve-year-old with a sword traveling with a green-clad hundred-year-old Nafia assassin.

"Just let me kill . . . ," Paddy wheezed. He stopped,

---

5 No, not Mafia. Nafia assassins spit on Mafia assassins and call them "salami slicers," an obscure sort of insult.

pulled a clear plastic respirator mask from his inside coat pocket, put it over his mouth and nose, and drew a deep breath. Then another.

And . . . another.

And . . .

. . . one more.

"Him," Paddy said finally, concluding the sentence which had begun, "Just let me kill."

Valin shook his head. "You are my mentor, Nine Iron, but this is a matter of family honor. First he must endure a hundred fiery stings!"

"As you . . . ," Paddy began.

And . . . breathed.

Okay, one more . . .

"Wish," Paddy concluded.

"Let me go!" Mack cried. He pulled at the chulks, but no, he wasn't pulling his way out of this one. The Brembles had him. Valin had him.

And the ants had him.

A second ant stung.

A third.

And now the stinging signal went out through all the ants.

Mack was about to die a most terrible death.

Really.

A fourth and fifth sting made Mack yell and thrash wildly. But now there was no more counting: the stings came fast and furious, a wave of them, pain upon pain, and already Mack felt himself swelling up, felt his airway constrict, felt his heart hammering way too fast, felt . . .

. . . felt death itself approaching, extending its bony claw to snuff the very life from him.

He pulled at the bony chulks, but each tug was weaker . . . weaker . . . until . . .

But before you're subjected to the awful details of the death of a heroic young boy, you should probably be told just how we got to this terrible situation.

So, for the moment just put that whole death-by-ant thing on hold. We'll get back to it. First we need to fill in a few details. Now, where were we when last we checked in with David "Mack" MacAvoy and the Magnificent Twelve?

I'll tell you where we were: we were in trouble. So much trouble you would not believe it. If we were to pause right here and explain all the many kinds of trouble Mack was in (not even counting the ants!), we would never be able to get on with the exciting (and deadly) conclusion of the story.

So we'll just do the short version.

In just a few days the Pale Queen would rise from her underground prison to destroy all freedom, crush all hope, deface all beauty, litter the landscape, cause the previously blemish-free to break out in unsightly pimples, and so terrorize the human race that even the bravest of folks (combat soldiers and sixth-grade teachers) would wet their pants in sheer, gibbering panic.

That's what the bravest of folks would do, but Mack was not counted among the bravest of folks. Mack had twenty-one identified phobias. Phobias are not regular fears; phobias are irrational fears. Crazy fears. So fearing the Pale Queen? That was not a phobia, that was just sensible. But being deathly afraid of beards? Well, that would be a phobia.

Mack had that fear of beards, which was called pogonophobia. Arachnophobia, a fear of spiders; dentophobia, a fear of dentists. And of course pupaphobia, a fear of puppets. Pyrophobia, which is a fear of fire; selachophobia—sharks; vaccinophobia,[6] a fear of shots.

A few others.

The worst of all the fears, the king of all fears, was claustrophobia, a fear of small, enclosed spaces. Small enclosed spaces that you're inside of. Like, say, a coffin. Or if someone locked you in a box.

Or a coffin.

People with claustrophobia really, really don't like coffins. Most people don't. But a person with claustrophobia will start sweating if you even just mention something like being buried alive.

I know! What a wimp, right?

And yet, to be shoved into a tiny space, unable to move your arms or legs, to feel yourself closed in, not enough air, all noise muffled, to hear perhaps the sound of dirt being shoveled onto . . .

So, maybe not so crazy, right?

Oddly enough, while Mack was afraid of all those things, he was not afraid of much else. He was irrationally terrified of many things but, no, Mack would not be among the wet-panted if he were to face the

---

6 Some book authors have that.

Pale Queen. If the Pale Queen had a beard,[7] then, sure, Mack would be paralyzed with fear. Or if she was carrying a shark. Otherwise, no. He was brave . . . except for where he was scared.

But isn't that the case with most of us?

Mack had been given a weighty task: he was to assemble a new Magnificent Twelve to face and defeat the Pale Queen. The first Magnificent Twelve had defeated the evil one three thousand years ago but had, sadly, given her a fixed sentence of banishment, which was now up. The Pale Queen was coming back, baby, and she was looking to bring the pain and the horror and the devastation and the utter ruin of the human race.

Why was a Magnificent Twelve needed? Couldn't the marines just deal with the Pale Queen?

No, they couldn't because the Pale Queen had powers beyond anything the marines could imagine. With her magic she could stop a bullet in midair. She could melt tanks. She could cause jets to go off course and fire their missiles at coffee shops. And she had minions, millions of them in a dozen evil species,

_____

7 She doesn't. Just a little down on her upper lip. You can barely see it.

from Skirrit to Bowands to treasonous Tong Elves to massive Gudridan. All of them would die for the Pale Queen. The marines were totally unprepared for the stuff she and her minions could do.

Plus, she had a secret weapon: her daughter, a goddess of evil who had troubled many civilizations down through history and earned many dark names. To the ancient Greeks she was Hecate. To the ancient Welsh she was Skatha. The Norse called her Hel, and the Norse knew what they were talking about. Her original name came from the most ancient of civilizations, which called her Ereskigal. She was known to Mack (and to you) as Risky.

Prior to his first encounter with Risky, Mack had never really noticed girls all that much. But she, in her evil way, had caused him to notice. Which was a terrible thing. When Risky was around, Mack would notice her quite a lot and then he would sweat and stammer and his voice would change and, basically, well, she had a disturbing effect on him.

Also, she was always trying to kill him, which definitely heightened the disturbance Mack felt. On the one hand, the unsettling effects of puberty; and on the other hand, attempted murder. It's just not a good combination no matter how you look at it.

The list of people trying to kill Mack was pretty impressive. Certainly Paddy "Nine Iron" Trout was trying to kill him. And so was Valin, his student. And so was Risky. And behind it all, her mother, the Pale Queen.

It was also the case that Thor had beefs with Mack.

Oh, and also William Blisterthöng MacGuffin.

Oh, and the Loch Ness Duck.

Oh, and the whole world had seen YouTube proof[8] that something very strange was going on with Mack, so the paparazzi were after him.

Oh, and *Le Bureau parisien de la gloire, la magnificence, et la défense de la langue française*[9] wanted Mack to put the Eiffel Tower back where it belonged. But only if he could do it in French.

You're probably getting the wrong impression now. Mack was a very nice person. Really.

On Mack's side he had the Magnifica, six of them

---

8 You can't get any proofier than YouTube.

9 The Parisian Office of Glory, Magnificence, and Defense of the French Language. Totally a real thing. But don't bother googling it, because they don't have a web page.

so far in addition to himself: Jarrah, Xiao, Dietmar, Sylvie, Rodrigo, and Charlie. They were from, respectively, Australia, China, Germany, France, Argentina, and Britain. Each was twelve years old. Each had the *enlightened puissance*. Each had learned at least a little of the magical Vargran tongue.

They'd been through some fights together, the seven existing Magnifica. They had been welded into a single, tight unit. They were like SEAL Team Six but without guns or muscles.

In addition to the Magnifica, Mack had Stefan. Stefan was the former King of All Bullies at Richard Gere Middle School[10] in Sedona, Arizona. But he had to give up bullying for bodyguarding. Stefan was not one of the Magnifica because, sadly, he did not possess the *enlightened puissance*. What he did possess was largeness, strength, scariness, and a total inability to be afraid.

He was also loyal to Mack. Mack had saved Stefan's life and so Mack was under Stefan's wing, by which Stefan meant that if you intended to hurt Mack, he would stop you—by any means necessary.

---

10 Go, Fighting Pupfish!

You may be wondering where Stefan is now that Valin has Mack staked out and ant-bitten. Good question. The answer will take a while. So strap yourself in and prepare yourself, because this is the story of the final confrontation between good and evil, between Mack and the Magnificent Twelve plus Stefan on the one hand and Risky, Paddy, a whole horde of creatures and monsters, and the Pale Queen herself on the other hand.

There will be terror.

There will be dragons.

There will be widespread devastation. Because I have to warn you: if your definition of a happy ending is that everyone lives happily ever after, well, this isn't going to end that way.

There is evil in the world, and evil always exacts a price from good.

TWO

"**W**e have to find the remaining four and some-how convince Valin to join us," Mack said. He was pacing thoughtfully up and down the suite at the Plaza Athénée hotel in Paris. It was quite a large suite and quite extravagantly beautiful. It was morning, so there were croissants and hot chocolate in silver service on the sideboard.

There were also croissant crumbs on the carpet and all three beds, and ditto hot-chocolate stains. This was the main boys' room—Mack, Dietmar, and Stefan had slept here. The secondary boys' room had been shared by Charlie and Rodrigo and was across the hall. The girls' suite was down one floor and had been enjoyed by Jarrah, Xiao, and Sylvie.

The two large suites cost 2,000 euros[11] each, while the smaller suite cost a mere 1,200 euros. Breakfast for seven cost just under 300 euros, which was kind of a lot, and given that they were spending 5,200 euros a night for the rooms, you'd have thought the Plaza Athénée would kick in a free breakfast. But no.

Fortunately Mack still had the special credit card with most of a million-dollar credit line.

There were gendarmes outside each of the three doors to the suite, but Mack wasn't too worried about evading them. If you can fight Risky to a draw, you can cope with a handful of French cops.

---

11 Euros are considered by some to be a type of money, a little bigger than a dollar.

Everyone was in the largest suite now, lounging on the beds, the sofas, the fancy chairs, and the floor—seven of the most important and powerful twelve-year-olds in human history. Plus Stefan, the world's most intimidating fifteen-year-old.

And they were all watching Mack pace thoughtfully. (Jarrah was watching suspiciously since it seemed to her that Mack kept pacing closer and closer to the last remaining croissant.)

"We need Grimluk," Dietmar said. "He will give us a clue to the remaining Magnifica."

"We've been here two and a half weeks, guys. I've spent a *lot* of time in the bathroom staring at the fixtures and I haven't seen him," Mack said.

Grimluk had a tendency to appear in shiny objects—sometimes mirrors, sometimes chrome bathroom fixtures.

"Maybe he is dead," Sylvie suggested. "It is the fate of all, is it not? We can perhaps delay the tolling of that final hour, and yet will it come."

Sylvie was philosophical. She was short and pretty and French with a sort of goth-emo look, and Mack found her fascinating. She was also Valin's half sister.

But not evil like him.

"Why should Grimluk die now?" Dietmar wondered. "He's lived for three thousand years."

"Who is this Grimluk bloke again?" Charlie asked. Charlie had only recently joined up, along with Rodrigo, and honestly, he sometimes didn't pay attention.

"One of the original Magnificent Twelve from three thousand years ago," Xiao explained. She was a patient person, Xiao was. Also not technically a person. She was looking very person-like at the moment, looking like a beautiful Chinese girl, but her true self was a dragon. Not a scary Western dragon—a more serpentine, turquoise, philosophical Chinese dragon. Like if the usual dragon matured and stopped trying to look all punk and took up reading books. "Grimluk has been Mack's guide from the start."

Rodrigo raised one elegant eyebrow. "Yes, so your guide—our guide—is a three-thousand-year-old man who speaks from bathrooms."

Jarrah said, "Mack, unless we have Valin, we'll never be the Twelve. We best go find that git and see if we can't change his mind." Jarrah was always about active verbs. *Go. Find. Jump. Yell. Smack. Fight.*

"I can change Valin's mind," Stefan said, and slammed his fist into the palm of his hand.

"We don't know where Valin is any more than we know where the remaining four Magnifica are," Mack said. "Last we saw of Valin, he was here in Paris. All we know is that whatever he has against me started sometime long, long ago in the Punjab."[12]

"Then let's go, right?" Jarrah said, and jumped up. Jarrah had been the first of the Magnifica to join Mack. She had her mother's dark skin and her father's blond hair and a wild recklessness that had absolutely captured Stefan's affection.

No one had a better idea, although Mack waited to hear one. He liked Paris. He liked this fancy hotel. He liked the fact that days had passed without anyone actively trying to kill him. But, nope, no one had a better idea. Darn it.

Thus it was that with croissant crumbs still unbrushed from their lips, the Magnificent Seven cast a quick Vargran spell on the gendarmes, who were caused, by virtue of this magic, to go en masse to the restaurant downstairs and order well-done steaks,[13]

12 See how we came back to the Punjab? Still no idea why it's *the* Punjab.
13 A misdemeanor in France.

allowing the Magnifica to escape.

You may be wondering: How does one get from Paris, France, to the Punjab? Well, first you find out that the largest city in the Indian Punjab is Amritsar, then you get onto Expedia and find out it's a twelve-hour flight and costs 5,139 US dollars if you're flying first class. And if you have a million-dollar credit card, why wouldn't you fly first class?

For once it would be an easy flight for Mack. He did not suffer from any flying-related phobias, so long as he wasn't flying over the ocean. Fly Mack over the ocean and you'd barely hear the in-flight movie over the sound of his chattering teeth, his weeping, his sudden panicky yelps, and the inevitable (but necessary) crunch of Stefan's knuckles against Mack's jaw, putting him to sleep.

Long story short, at ten a.m. the next day they stepped, well-rested (hey, first class, remember?), into the Amritsar airport. They were met by the guide Mack had arranged in advance. This turned out to be a man in a purple turban and an amazing beard named Singh. The man, not the beard. Or the turban.

To clarify, neither the beard nor the turban was named Singh, but the tour guide was.

It didn't matter, because Singh's beard was a major beard. It was glossy black, and curled up inside itself into a sort of concentrated, extra-strength beard.

"Ah ah ah!" Mack cried, and backpedaled away, crashing into the living dead (the people who had flown coach), who snarled angrily as they pushed past, dragging their squalling children and diaper bags.

"What's the matter?" Rodrigo demanded. He was a sophisticated kid and did not like being embarrassed in public.

"Oh, my goodness: beard!"[14] Jarrah said. Jarrah knew most of Mack's little "issues."

"Ah ah ah ah!" Mack continued to cry.

And then . . . then he looked around. It was as if scales had fallen from his eyes, and he saw, truly saw, that he was surrounded by beards. Beards and turbans, but the turbans were rather attractive, really, coming as they did in a wide array of colors. But beards . . . beards were a problem.

This might as well have been the annual beard convention. The percentage of people with beards here was greater than the percentage of Civil War generals with beards. And these were not ironic, hipster beards,

---

14 In Australian it's pronounced "bee-yud."

but full-on, glossy black beards.

Mack had slept most of the way on the plane and when he wasn't sleeping he was playing video games on the in-flight entertainment system. (In first class they let you win all the games.) So he had not noticed that about half the men (and some of the women) on the flight had beards.

But now, as he looked around, eyes darting, breath coming short and fast, heart beating like a gerbil who'd fallen into a silo of coffee beans and had to eat his way out, he realized beards . . . terrifying beards . . . were everywhere.

The Punjab was the home office of beards!

Stefan made a grab for Mack but missed, and Mack went screaming off through the crowd, bouncing like a pinball from one nonplussed traveler to the next.

Singh said, "Perhaps your friend has jet lag?"

"Nah, he's just crazy," Jarrah said, but affectionately.

Stefan sighed and raced after Mack and finally tackled him, hefted him onto his shoulder, walked toward the men's room, and as he passed Jarrah said, "Maybe a swirlie will calm him down."

As a former bully, Stefan had a limited imagination when it came to problem solving. There was pretty much:

1) Threatening.

2) Punching.

3) Dunking someone's head in a toilet (swirlie).

Mack was still yelling like a madman when Stefan slammed him—as gently as he could—against the men's room wall and said, "Do I have to punch you? Or will a swirlie do it?"

Mack's breath was coming in short, panicky gasps. But he had stopped screaming, which was good.

"Get a grip," Stefan said, using his lowest level of threatening voice. It was almost kind. Not really, but for him.

"You don't understand. I—I-I-I . . ."

Stefan let him go, and Mack, still shaking, tried to get a grip. What he gripped was the sink. He stared at his reflection in the mirror. He didn't look good, frankly. He looked old—really, really old. He had wrinkles that looked like an aerial map of the Rocky Mountains. His teeth were tinged green. His hair was pale and wispy. His eyes were unfocused, blank, wandering randomly around like he was following two agitated flies simultaneously.

In fact, he looked exactly like Grimluk.

"Grimluk!" Mack cried. Because it was true: the reflection was no reflection at all but the familiar, astoundingly old, grizzled, gamy, quite-possibly-somewhat-dead face of Grimluk.

"I fade. . . . Mack of the Magnifica . . . I weaken. . . ."

"Oh no you don't!" Mack snapped. "You just got here!"

Grimluk blinked. "Oh? It felt like longer. Where are you?"

"The Punjab!"

"Hmmm. I don't know that one," Grimluk said. "In my day we only had seven countries: Funguslakia, North Rot, Crushia, the Republic of Stench, Scabia, Eczema, and Delaware."

"I don't care. Grimluk, I'm trying to find Valin and solve whatever his problem is. Plus I still have to figure out who the others are. You have to help!"

"Others?"

"I only have six with me: Jarrah, Xiao, Dietmar, Sylvie, Charlie, and Rodrigo."

"Just eight?"

"No, that's seven total, counting me. We still need Valin and four more."

"Are you sure?"

"Yes. Yes. I can do basic math!"

Grimluk drew himself up with as much dignity as he could while peering out of a smeared bathroom mirror and said, "There is no need to flaunt your fancy modern learning. I fade. . . . I weaken. . . . I was never . . . good . . . at math. . . ."

"Where do I find Valin and the other four?"

"Not in the same place, Mack."

At this point Stefan said, "You're talking to the old dude I can't see, right?"

Stefan's remark caused Mack to look around and take notice of the fact that three very polite tourists from Japan were taking video of what looked like a crazy kid talking—yelling, actually—at a mirror.

"I'm not crazy," Mack said. No one was convinced.

"Valin is near, though he won't be when you catch him," Grimluk said. "The others . . . the others . . ."

And sure enough, the image faded, and the ancient voice—a voice so old that when Grimluk spoke, you could practically hear wrinkles—likewise faded out.

"Nooooo!" Mack pounded the mirror because now his own reflection had appeared, replacing Grimluk's.

Grimluk faded back in. "A gate . . ."

"A what?"

"Golden . . . of . . . I see a pillar of orange. . . ."

"No, no, no, none of that cryptic stuff," Mack yelled. "We are running out of time!"

"Ants!" Grimluk cried.

"What?"

"Beware of ants!"

"I promise I will," Mack yelled. "Now just tell me how to find—"

"I see a bridge of orange. . . ."

"What?"

"Actually more of a . . . I fade. . . . I weaken. . . ."

"Get back here!"

"Reddish orange. A gate of gold."

And with that, he was gone.

"Grimluk!" Mack howled.

Making a "grrrrrr" face, Mack stormed out of the bathroom, to find the others talking to Singh. Mack kept his distance. In his present state of mind, eight feet felt like the minimum beard-clearance zone. Probably when he calmed down he'd start feeling a little better about it. But right now his head was swimming and he was tired and he was on edge.

And that was when things got really bad. Because as Mack was turning Grimluk's insane, rambling, incoherent, nonsensical, senile words over and over again in his head, a massive, glittering, impossible wall of steel came crashing down through the roof, down through the huge slanted windows, down through the vegetarian restaurant, down through the adjacent and fortunately unoccupied boarding area.

It missed Mack by nine inches and cut him off from his friends.

Ker-RAAAAASH!

Followed by, *Bam! Screeeeech! Tinkle, tinkle, tinkle.* And screams!

The noise was deafening. Broken glass, twisted aluminum rafters, screams, cries. It sounded like the end of the world punctuated with an earthshaking impact that hit so hard Mack felt as if the floor had attacked his feet. (He was not at his most rational, just then.)

The wall of steel had come down like a guillotine or a meat cleaver. It sliced right across the airport. Mack's frantic, terrified glances did not show anyone around him killed—thankfully—but the restaurant was destroyed, the kitchen shattered, and indeed globs of *sarson da saag*[15] struck Mack in the cheek.

He looked, sickened with fear, at the place where the blade bit into the floor. He did not see any body parts there. That was a good thing. His thoughts had gone straight to Sylvie, for some reason, but he did not see her hands or head lying separated from the rest of her.

"Huh," Stefan remarked from the opposite side of the steel wall.

Just as quickly and noisily as it had come slashing down, the wall of steel pulled back up, revealing a deep gash right across the airport.

Through the chasm in the roof Mack saw that the steel wall was in fact an impossibly huge blade. And he saw that said blade was the blade of a terrifyingly large scimitar.

And he further saw that holding that huge scimitar was a massive hand, a hand the size of a middle school multipurpose room. The fingers were detailed with rings of gold, some with rubies the size of Subarus.

Not surprisingly, there was an arm. You'd expect that arm to be large, and it was; oh, it definitely was.

---

15 Surely you know this is a favorite curry dish from the Punjab.

But by the time Mack's eyes traveled from scimitar to hand to arm, he was more taken by the bare chest as wide as a football field and, beyond, way up in the air, fifty feet or more above the airport, a head.

How big was the head? Have you ever seen the Macy's Thanksgiving parade with the giant helium-filled floats of, like, Spider-Man? Okay, imagine a pumpkin. Now imagine an evil, supervillain pumpkin so big that if it was a helium-filled float it would make helium-filled Spidey say, "Whoa!"

That's how big.

There was only one good thing about that gigantic head atop that gigantic body: it did not have a beard. It was a bit young for a beard.

In another odd sort of detail, there was a man in the pocket of the giant's vest. Yes, the giant was so large that a man could stand in his vest pocket.

That pocketed man was dressed all in green.

"Ha!" the giant roared. "HA!" In a voice that caused decorative flags to tear loose from their poles. "I've got you now, Mack!"

The giant was Valin. And you've already guessed the name of the man in his pocket.[16]

---

16 Paddy "Nine Iron" Trout. Pay attention; I can't keep giving you answers.

Three

MEANWHILE, 7,831 MILES AWAY, IN SEDONA, ARIZONA

The golem was at a dance with Camaro Angianelli. The golem was a creature . . . well, that seems harsh, doesn't it? Referring to someone as a creature? Let's take another run at that. The golem was a . . . being. A person, even, made of mud and twigs and magically infused with life and a sense of purpose by the placement in his mouth of a tiny scroll bearing two words: *Be Mack.*

Grimluk had created the golem to cover for Mack while Mack was off trying to save the world.

Despite the fact that the golem had a tendency to wash away in the rain, and occasionally would grow or shrink in unpredictable ways, and turned in history papers with titles like "What Color Was the Sky in 1812? Green?" no one had discovered his secret.

No one, at least, until Camaro Angianelli figured out that something was very odd about this not-quite-Mack.

Camaro had recently been promoted to Queen of All Bullies at Richard Gere Middle School.[17] She had been anointed queen when Tony Pooch, her last competition for the job, had run from a fight with her. Of course if Stefan came back, she would have no choice but to return the title of Bully Supreme to him—even Camaro didn't want to have to take on Stefan. But for now Camaro was riding high. She had appointed many new sub-bullies, changing the categories to keep up with the times. For example, the category of "nerd" was now combined with "dork" and they had a single bully. (Geeks had been exempted from bullying after paying Camaro a bribe in the form of cheat codes to Halo 4.)

17 Go, Fighting Pupfish!

Preppies had disappeared altogether, to be replaced by hipsters.

Twilight fans were assigned a new bully—the old one had been found actually reading one of the books,[18] which was totally against the spirit of things.

Camaro had also brought a new level of humaneness to the organized bully system that Stefan had created. For example, she had set limits on the amount of lunch money that could be extorted (20 percent for most kids, 40 percent for rich kids).

More revolutionary still, Camaro had created the brand-new position of Popular Mean Girls Bully. The PMGs had never liked Camaro, and Camaro could hold a grudge. The Popular Mean Girls' bully, whose name was Jennifer Schwarz, was not especially big or strong, but she made up for it by being incredibly obnoxious and absolutely relentless. She bullied through nagging and refusing to go away, and it was quite effective. In fact, Jennifer Schwarz had set up a nice little business on the side selling the lip gloss, earrings, and cell phone skins she extorted from the PMGs.

Anyway, before we got distracted by the politics

---

18 And whispering, "Choose Jacob, he's awesome!"

of bullying, we were at a dance. Camaro was a pretty good dancer. The golem was . . . Hmmm. Well, as a dancer, the golem was . . . What's a good word? He was . . . original. Yes, original. For one thing, he took up a fair amount of room when he danced. In fact, it was best to stay at least ten feet back because the flailing, falling, plunging, and temporary body-part loss could endanger innocent bystanders.

Everyone kind of liked the way he could dance up the walls, but most folks thought dancing on the ceiling was just show-offy. And, too, he yelped at odd times.

But no one said anything or even looked at him funny because he was Camaro's boyfriend. And in case it isn't clear by now, Camaro was not a girl you messed with. For her part, she liked the golem's exuberance. She alone knew that he was not really Mack. She alone knew that there was something supernatural about him. And that he had secrets. And that he could, if controlled by the wrong person, become very, very dangerous.

Risky had placed a cell phone in the golem's mouth at one point hoping to use texts to reprogram the golem from playing the part of Mack to becoming the Destroyer.

Camaro had put a stop to that. But she was not foolish enough to believe that Risky was done with the golem.

For now, though, it was all good from her point of view. In fact, Camaro was having a really nice time dancing with the golem.

Happiness. Warm, sweet, gentle happiness.

But how long was that going to last with the Pale Queen nearing the date when she would emerge to trouble all of humanity?

Not long, that's how long.

Camaro looked out over her queendom, out at the two hundred or so kids—some dancing, most standing awkwardly and gawping, or staring fixedly down at their smartphones—and it was then she noticed that some of the kids were unfamiliar to her.

Some were kid-sized in terms of tallness, but broader, thicker, more muscular, and very strangely dressed in lederhosen.[19]

Now that she noticed, some of the chaperones were

---

19 Google it. Seriously, you gotta see what lederhosen look like.

a little unusual, too. They had a distinctly insect-like aspect to them. As if the moms and dads had been replaced by large grasshoppers wearing human clothing.

Camaro stopped dancing, although the golem kept right on. Her eyes narrowed and she cracked her knuckles just the way Stefan would have.

Something disturbing was happening in the queendom of Camaro Angianelli. She didn't yet know of the treasonous Tong Elves, who, coincidentally, were about the size of middle-schoolers but broader, thicker, creepier, and more muscular, and very strangely dressed.

Nor did she know of the foul Skirrit species with their unwholesome similarity to grasshoppers.

But she soon would.

She took three bold steps, yanked the golem down off the wall, pinned his arms so he would stop flailing (dancing), and said, "Give me your phone: I need to talk to Mack."

Four

There was a time when a hundred-foot-tall twelve-year-old with a scimitar and a Nafia hit man in his pocket would have scared Mack.

But Mack had learned a few things. He'd been in a few fights. He'd stood up to Skirrit, Tong Elves, Lepercons, even Gudridan. He'd been yanked out of a jet over the South Pacific. He'd been fired through the air by a crazy old Scotsman.

Most of all: after much stalling, he'd actually finally studied some Vargran from the Vargran Key.

The giant Valin raised his scimitar, this time

shifting his grip so that rather than readying to bring it down in a broad sweeping cut he could stab it down, point first. Valin could see Mack now; he could see him through the hole in the roof, and his beef was specifically with Mack.

He wasn't an indiscriminate killer, after all. He wanted to kill Mack, not a bunch of innocent airline passengers.

"*Lom-ma poindra!*" Mack cried.

Why did he yell that? Because those are the Vargran words for "disappear sword!" In the imperative, or "or else!" tense that is unique to Vargran.

Mack was pretty sure this would work, so he was upset when instead of disappearing, the gigantic scimitar came stabbing straight down at him.

He jumped back, tripped, fell on his butt, and had to scoot away like a dog on a carpet.

The point of the scimitar hit the floor, threw up a spray of broken tile, and plunged clear down through the floor into the underlying dirt.

"What the heck?" Mack asked.

Valin yanked the weapon skyward again. "It's not a sword, moron," Valin said in a giant voice. "It's a scimitar!"

Yes. Well, it was a scimitar, which is a kind of sword, but Vargran spells do require some specificity.

And now Mack could feel that in his panic he had used up his *enlightened puissance*. He felt the emptiness, the slight sadness (slight because sadness has a hard time competing with terror) that came from the expenditure of power.

Down came the swor— the scimitar.

Mack was so upset he didn't even move. Fortunately Stefan was not so depressed. He ran, took a flying leap, and hit Mack like a sixteen-pound (the largest size) bowling ball knocking into one wobbly pin.

"Oooof!"

Followed by, *ker-RAAASH!*

It was a close call. The scimitar passed so near that it actually sliced through the tail of Mack's T-shirt. Had Stefan been even a millisecond slower, Mack would have been impaled. He would never have survived long enough to have ants bite his eyeballs.

"Thanks," Mack gasped. He shot a look at his stunned fellow Magnifica and yelled, "A little help?"

Dietmar was quickest to respond. "What is the word for scimitar?"

"Never mind the sword, go after Valin!" Jarrah

said, which was a pretty reasonable suggestion, especially since Mack was now running to get out of Valin's line of sight.

Ker-RASH!

Down came the scimitar again.

"Give up, Mack! Surrender before innocent people are hurt!" Valin cried in a voice that rattled the shattered glass like BBs on a drum.

Mack had ducked under a bench. He was gasping for breath, looking beseechingly at his friends. Really: time for them to do something, because maybe Valin couldn't see him here but he could still randomly—

Ker-RASH!

The scimitar came stabbing down through a previously undestroyed section of the airport, and this time the point landed just between two little kids. Neither was hurt, but it was too close. Too close by far.

"Okay, stop!" Mack yelled. "Stop. I'll surrender!"

He rolled out from under the bench. Mack held up his hands.

It was Xiao—she was always a studious one—who came up with just the right Vargran spell. But she knew she'd need help to pull off something this hard.

So as Mack was holding up his hands and Stefan

was glaring helplessly up at giant Valin, Xiao joined hands with Jarrah, Charlie, and Sylvie—it felt like a spell that four people could manage—and together they chanted, "*A-ma Mack exel-i Valin.*"

Or in English: "Make Mack bigger than Valin."

Yeah. Bigger.

They did not specify a time frame. So it happened with remarkable speed. One second Mack was holding his hands up in surrender, and about three seconds later those hands hit the ceiling of the airport and pushed it up and literally tipped it right off. The airport at Amritsar is a simple rectangle, with a lid-like roof atop plate glass windows, so the roof came away almost as a single piece, a huge steel-and-glass rectangle.

You thought the noise of the scimitar was loud? This was even louder, because all the way around the roof were steel beams held in place by thick rivets and welds, and breaking all that was noisy.

But break it Mack did, and as he rose, as he grew, as he soared high up into the air, he pushed the roof off. It crashed atop a parked jet—empty aside from the cleaning crew, who managed to survive by cramming into the tiny bathroom.

Mack grew and grew. It was a painless process, but

a potentially embarrassing one since Mack's clothing was human-sized. He was concerned he might have a sort of Incredible Hulk clothing issue, but, fortunately for all concerned, his clothing grew along with him.

There was quite a view from a hundred feet up. Mack saw farm fields, and a small city, and the bigger city of Amritsar off to the south.

He also saw a small private jet coming in for a landing and flying directly toward him right around eye level. The pilot was staring with disbelieving eyes, too transfixed by the bizarreness of two gigantic twelve-year-olds to steer away.

Mack dodged aside, ducking low, which was very good luck because at that very moment Valin swung his scimitar horizontally as if he meant to cut off Mack's head.[20]

The scimitar passed harmlessly over Mack's head but sliced the tail right off the private plane.

This was bad. The reason planes have a tail is that it allows them to turn. Also it keeps them from either pitching straight down to the ground or straight up in the air and actually falling over backward and then heading straight for the ground.

---

20 He did mean to.

That's what happened.

"Hey!" Mack yelled. "The plane!"

But Valin was already preparing for a second scimitar swing.

Mack made a desperate snatch for the plane. It was very strange, like trying to grab a badminton shuttlecock in midair. He learned something surprising: like the feathers of a badminton shuttlecock, actual airplane wings aren't all that strong if you grab them with a giant fist.

He also learned: jet engines are really hot.

"Ahhh!" he yelled.

The three passengers on the jet also yelled, "Ahhh!" but with an Indian accent.

Mack swung with the direction of the jet, trying desperately not to crush it as it went from two hundred miles an hour to zero miles an hour in a single second.

The scimitar swung!

Too late to duck!

"*(Ch)on-ma Mack i poindrafol!*" was shouted with a German accent.

Dietmar!

In a millisecond a huge shield appeared in the air

between Mack and the flashing scimitar.

CLANNNNNNNG!

The blade bit into the shield but not through. Instantly Mack slid his forearm into the straps of the shield, even as he carefully held the jet with his other hand. He knelt, laid the jet on the ground—upside down, but hey, it was better than crashing.

Valin was breathing hard—swinging a scimitar the size of a sequoia isn't easy, especially if you're not a practiced swordsman.

Mack, for his part, stuck his now-giant fingers into his giant mouth and winced at the pain from the jet exhaust.

"What is your problem?" Mack yelled at Valin, mumbling because of the fingers in his mouth.

"There is bad blood between our two families!" Valin cried.

Paddy "Nine Iron" Trout wheezed, "Yes, an ancient blood feud of . . ."

He reached for his oxygen bottle, but Mack was not in the mood to wait politely.

"Whatever it was, I apologize, all right?" Mack said.

"Ah, so you admit that your great-great-great . . ." This went on for a while, so for brevity's sake let's just cut to: ". . . great-grandfather dishonored my family and destroyed my ancestry!"

"What the . . . Look, I don't even—"

"My ancestors swore to Guru Hargobind himself that they would never rest until the insult was—"

"Guru Hargobind?"

"Aha! So you do know! And so, you die!"

Valin stabbed at Mack and missed, but dodging had put Mack off balance. He would not be able to avoid the next sweep of that terrible sword.

Suddenly a new creature appeared on the scene. It was as big as Mack and as big as Valin. But this giant was Stefan—magicked into existence by the combined Vargran efforts of three of the Magnifica below.

"Give me that," Stefan growled to Mack, and yanked the shield from his arm.

Valin raised the scimitar high as if to strike at Stefan, but Stefan wasn't having it. Not even a little. He raised the shield over his head and charged straight at Valin like an enraged bull, yelling, "Gaaaahhhhh!"

Valin swallowed hard, clapped a protective hand

over Paddy "Nine Iron," still peeking out of his pocket, and ran away, waving the scimitar ineffectually over his shoulder. "This is not over! I will force you to face your guilt!"

Huge Mack and huge Stefan stared at each other.

"Should I go after him?" Stefan asked.

"No. We've already destroyed the airport. We could end up crushing cars and houses."

"Huh," Stefan said, and he was not happy about it. Most likely because he had always been a great admirer of Godzilla and would have relished crushing some houses with Mack.

But Mack had a better idea. He looked down at tiny Xiao and said, "That treaty that says you can't be your dragon self in the lands of Western dragons . . ."

Xiao nodded, grinned, and said, "This is no longer the West."

In seconds she had left behind her human form and taken on her own, true form as a wingless turquoise Chinese dragon. She slithered into the air—a remark-able thing to see—and, flying low to the ground to avoid being spotted by Valin, went after him and the Nafia assassin.

EVEN LONGER AGO THAN EVER BEFORE

The Pale Queen had been feared and worshipped since human beings first learned to walk erect. In fact, the Pale Queen had helped that process along. Anytime she saw an early human—whether it was a *Homo erectus*, a *Homo habilis*, or even a *Homo neanderthalensis*—who was leaning too far forward or knuckle-walking, she would say, "Hey! Stand up straight!" And if they didn't, she'd kill them with an energy bolt or by dropping rocks on their heads.

She was like a very strict teacher.

After many, many years of this, there weren't all that many early humans knuckle-walking anymore. Standing fully upright turned out to make a lot of sense in terms of survival.

The Pale Queen needed early humans to walk upright because that would free their hands to do the important work of writing about the Pale Queen, building temples for the Pale Queen, and sacrificing sheep and maidens to the Pale Queen. It took her quite a while to get humans to that point, and her efforts earned her a lot of respect in the primitive ancient cities of Ur of the Chaldees, Nineveh of the Assyrians, Sumer of the Akkadians, and Indianapolis of the Pacers.

But when Babylon came along, the Babylonians chilled the Pale Queen. The Babylonians thought they were all that, and they saw the Pale Queen as being last year's model when it came to godding. So there was no temple to the Pale Queen, and no cult of shaved-headed priests, and no sheep or maidens being sacrificed.

Which was totally unacceptable to the Pale Queen.

But you know how kids are supposed to help around the house? How they are supposed to have a list of chores and just do them without being nagged ten times? Well, same thing in the Pale Queen's house. Her daughter expected to have everything handed to her: goddess robes, flying sandals, chariots drawn by unicorns, parties with her friends (she had no friends), and she didn't want to have to do any of the work.

"Listen to me, young lady, I'm giving you a chore to do. You will make the Babylonians worship me. I want a main temple and two smaller—"

"Why are you picking on me?" Risky demanded.

"I'm not picking on you. I'm telling you what I want you to do."

Heavy sigh. "Okay, what? Gáh!"

"I want a main temple and two smaller ones. The main one has to be bigger than Astarte's. I want a cult. I want sacrifices. And I want some kind of invocation."

"What's an invocation? Am I supposed to know that?"

The Pale Queen gritted her thirty-six teeth because Risky was grinding her last nerve. "An invocation is like when someone says, 'Praise Astarte!' or 'Zeus, that hurt!' or, 'Where the Baal are my keys?' That kind of thing."

So Risky rolled her eyes and promised to do it next millennium. But the Pale Queen wasn't having it and insisted her daughter get out right now, young lady, and get started.

So verily did Risky go forth into the land of Babylon. Babylon was watered by two rivers, the Tigris and the Euphrates. In those very early days Babylon was still a bit scruffy. Some of the best buildings were made of stone, but a lot were just mud smeared over sticks.

Risky was walking through the ox-poop-strewn streets, threading her way past lepers and refusing offers of souvenirs from the many shopkeepers.

And then she saw him.

Yes, him.

He was the strongest, handsomest, most armored-up guy she had ever seen in her life.

To be honest, Risky hadn't dated much during the first thousand years of her existence. What human males she had even seen had been in the process of being eaten by her mother. Or occasionally by Risky herself. And it's hard to get a good impression of a guy who is crying and begging for his life, only to be gobbled up.

This, however, was different.

He was tall. His hair was lustrous black. His armor glittered silver and gold in the sunlight. He had almost all of his teeth and he did not smell like a goat, which was pretty rare in Babylon. The concept of hotness had not yet been invented, but if it had been, Risky would have said he was hot.

Risky stopped in the middle of the street and stared. She did not know how to play it cool. Like hotness, cool had also not yet been invented, so people just pretty much acted however they felt and expressed their emotions openly.

These were very primitive times.

"Why are you staring at me?" the young man asked.

"Because your hands are as gold rings set with beryl," Risky said. "Your belly is as bright ivory overlaid with sapphires. Your legs are as pillars of marble set upon sockets of fine gold. Your countenance is as Lebanon, excellent as the cedars, and your mouth is most suh-weet."

Somehow the sight of this boy was making Risky go weak in the knees but strong in the similes. She knew she was babbling. She knew it was crazy, but it was how she felt. She felt smitten. She felt gobsmacked. She felt . . . love.

"I like your hair," the boy said. "You have the hair of a goddess."

"I am a goddess," Risky pointed out. "See?" To demonstrate, she transformed into a huge beast made up of the useful parts of a lion, a bear, a ram, and a bull. But she kept the hair through the whole thing.

The boy turned and ran, but Risky bounded on

her powerful kangaroo legs (yeah, kangaroo, too) and smacked him down on his back. She landed atop him and once again became her usual amazingly attractive self.

"What's your name, human boy?"

"G-G-G-G-Gil."

"G-G-G-G-Gil?"

He swallowed hard and said, "Gil. Gil Gamesh."

"Epic," she said approvingly. She jumped up effortlessly and pulled him to his feet. "I need to build a temple for the Pale Queen."

"The Pale Queen?" Gil echoed. He frowned. "But isn't she evil?"

"Oh, she's evil all right," Risky said with airy dismissal.

"I heard she demanded a human sacrifice of a thousand Amalekites."

Risky spread her hands and smiled. "They were out of goats."

"Will she demand human sacrifices here in Babylon?"

"That depends. How fast do you think we can get a temple built?"

Oh, the days that followed were magical for Risky. She and Gil chose an architect for the temple. Then they picked out draperies and looked at paint samples and interviewed potential priests. There were so many details: whether to have pews or just make everyone stand, whether they would have music—possibly bleating horns—which knives to use to cut the throats of sacrifices, whether the blood would be caught in copper bowls or silver bowls. (Both were hard to keep polished, but this "bronze" everyone was talking about struck them both as too newfangled.)

Gil took one job for himself, keeping it coyly secret from Risky: finding a sculptor for the great statue of the Pale Queen that would dominate the altar.

The more they worked together, the more they liked each other. They held hands. They gazed into each other's eyes. Gil even wrote her poetry.

> *Your neck is like a gazelle's,*
> *You're good at magic and spells,*
> *Your skin is fair,*
> *I like your hair,*
> *When I look at you my heart swells.*

No one said it was great poetry. Gil was just starting out as a writer and poet. He was actually much better at sword fighting than writing. But he was also very organized and had a way of getting things done that sometimes surprised Risky. When it was time to form the bricks for the temple's foundation, Risky suggested sending a conquering army to enslave the Canaanites and use their blood to mix with the mortar.

Gil came up with a totally different approach: he simply hired some professional bricklayers and used water to mix with the mortar.

"You're so efficient," Risky gushed.

The girl was smitten.

And so was Gil.

Their love burned hot for a while. But that which burns hottest often burns out quickest. Like a match that flares in the darkness only to be extinguished by the smallest breeze.

And when love dies . . .

Five

Mack and Stefan had been shrunk back to normal size again by the time Xiao returned to report that Valin had likewise shrunk upon reaching Amritsar.

"Did you see where he went? Would you be able to find it again?" Mack asked her as she shifted back to human shape.

"Easily. He and Paddy went into the Golden Temple."

"The what now?"

60

At this point they were outside the airport, completely surrounded by khaki-uniformed men wearing khaki turbans and carrying nightsticks. These were Amritsar police. There was also a swiftly growing number of men in camouflage uniforms, some in turbans, some in berets, all armed with rifles. These were Indian military.

Beyond the ring of threatening police and military forces were regular folks with cell phones taking pictures. And somehow paparazzi were there clicking away from behind superlong lenses.

None of this worried Mack very much. First of all, he was done worrying about YouTube. It was just a given that they would be starring in yet another viral video.

And the armed men weren't a great concern because, frankly, at this point the Magnificent Seven had more than enough Vargran to deal with mere humans. Indeed, Sylvie, Jarrah, and Charlie had combined to freeze the armed men in place, which was why Mack was not handcuffed and on his way to jail.

This meant that all the beards on all those armed

men were also frozen in place. This definitely made them less terrifying. After all, a beard at rest will stay at rest, while a beard in motion may run right into you at some point.[21]

Dietmar had his phone out and was googling the "Golden Temple." Actually he pronounced it "golten," with a *t*. It irritated Mack, as most things about Dietmar did.

"It is a temple belonging to the Sikh religion," Dietmar reported.

"Oy, don't be calling someone's religion sick," Charlie said.

"*Sikh* not *sick*," Dietmar explained.

"You're doing it again?" Charlie demanded.

Xiao put a calming hand on his arm. Charlie needed a calming hand because he had been pretty shaken up seeing Xiao first turn into a dragon and then turn back into a girl. There was a lot of weirdness to being part of the Magnificent Twelve. He was one of the newer members and he'd already had to get used to a lot.

"Sikh. S-I-K-H," Xiao spelled it out.

---

21 Newton's fourth law.

"Yeah," Jarrah said, like she'd known it all along. (She hadn't.)

"In fact, most of these fellows around us with the beards are Sikhs," Dietmar pointed out.

"Yes, this is true." This from Singh, whose reappearance made them all jump. Mack was adjusted to the fact that all the closest beards were spell-frozen. Singh had been out of range and he now threaded his way carefully through the rows of poised and motionless soldiers and police.

"No closer!" Mack cried, and covered his eyes. "No offense. I have a phobia about beards."

"So you came to the Punjab?" Singh asked skeptically. "If you have a phobia of sharks, do you go swimming in the ocean?"

"Please don't say *shark*!" Mack begged.

"What's this Golden Temple, then?" Jarrah asked, trying to move past the awkwardness.

"It is a place very sacred to our religion," Singh said.

"Then how come they let Valin in?" Mack demanded through his fingers. "I mean, even if he's a Sikh, I don't think Nine Iron is."

Singh shrugged. (Not that Mack could see this.)

And he said, "All faiths, all races, all sexes, everyone is welcome. Plus: free lunch."

"I'd kill for a burger," Stefan said at the mention of lunch.

Singh shook his head. (Again, this was lost on Mack.) "No, sir, we are vegetarian." Then, seeing the blank look on Stefan's face, he expanded. "We do not eat flesh. The meal would perhaps be lentils."

"I'd kill for a lentil," Stefan said.

"Is there anything you wouldn't kill for?" Rodrigo asked. Like Charlie, he was still somewhat new to the Magnificent Twelve.

"Brussels sprouts," Stefan said without hesitation, and the pure, distilled hatred in his voice convinced Mack that no matter where else they went, they should never go to Belgium.[22]

"Could Valin stay in the temple?" Mack asked.

"Not for long," Singh said. "It's a very busy place."

"Okay then," Mack said forcefully, or as forcefully as he could under the circumstances. "We go after Valin. Then: San Francisco."

"Why San Francisco?" Sylvie asked.

---

22 Because Brussels is in Belgium, see. Get it? Never mind.

Mack shrugged. "Grimluk said something about an orange bridge, then he said it was more of a rust red. And he mentioned a golden gate. That would have to be the Golden Gate Bridge in San Francisco."

"So first the Golden Temple, and then the Golden Gate," Sylvie said. "If only we could be sure that our futures were so golden."

Sylvie didn't know it yet, but she was right to harbor such doubts. She was in a quandary, Sylvie was. Valin was her half brother. And Mack, well, she had come to care about Mack. Of course Mack was blithely unaware that she had a *tendre*[23] for him, or that however much she despised what Valin was doing, she still had to hope he would not be hurt.

"Will any of us survive?" Sylvie asked herself quietly. "Will loyalty or love mean anything in the end? Is it true, as Sartre said, that life begins on the other side of despair?"

Yep, she was philosophical, Sylvie was. She watched Mack slithering away atop Xiao's rippling turquoise back and felt momentarily abandoned. Jarrah was feeling much the same, gazing after Stefan.

---

23 French for a crush.

The two girls' hands touched, and they offered each other a silent, reassuring squeeze.

Riding off with the wind in his face and Stefan's knees in his back, Mack heard his phone ring. He didn't answer it for fear he would drop it, and how was he going to replace a phone in the middle of all this?

He made a mental note to check for messages as soon as he landed, but he forgot, and so he did not receive Camaro's worried voice mail.

Thus was Richard Gere Middle School[24] doomed.

---

24 I don't even have the heart to say, "Go, Fighting Pupfish."

Six

MEANWHILE, 7,831 MILES AWAY,
IN SEDONA, ARIZONA

"**H**e's not answering," Camaro said, staring at the phone like she might smash it.

The golem was continuing to dance, but he was dancing on the floor, which was a good thing. "Maybe Mack's dancing."

(Mack was not dancing, as you know perfectly well. He was riding a dragon toward the Golden Temple of Amritsar.)

Camaro's eyes narrowed suspiciously. "There's something very wrong here tonight. The question is: What do we do about it?"

"Leave a message?" the golem suggested, which was a pretty sensible suggestion. It surprised Camaro: the golem was not always[25] sensible.

"Mack, it's Camaro. Something very weird is going on here. There's a bunch of creepy short dudes and a bunch of locust-looking people, too. Call me."

She hung up the call, gave the phone back to the golem, and thought. Camaro might be a bit of a thug but she was not stupid. In fact she had good grades and had a particular knack for math and science. She could think when she needed to.

And she could observe, too. At this particular moment she was observing the fact that all the stocky little dudes and the buggy creatures were watching the golem.

So. They were there for the golem. This was about him, and, Camaro intuited, about that red-haired girl the golem had told her about. She was the one who'd almost caused the golem to kill Camaro.

Uncool.

---

25 Or ever.

Camaro searched the room for the redhead, but she wasn't there. She wasn't the kind of girl you easily overlooked.

"So these are just minions," Camaro muttered, and nodded knowingly. Minions were like underbullies. There might be a lot of them, but if old James Bond movies, Bruce Willis movies, and Star Wars movies had taught her anything, it was that minions are easily disposed of.

She sidled up to Tony Pooch, who flinched at her approach. "Bully emergency. Keep it quiet. Spread the word."

She did the same with Ed Lafrontiere, the disgraced *Twilight* fans' bully, who was now hoping for a new assignment. And Matthew Morgan, who dealt with nerds and dorks.

Within seconds the word had gone out to all twelve official bullies—and Disgraced Ed. They gathered around Camaro and the golem.

"Listen up," Camaro said. "I am declaring this an official bully emergency. You are all bound by the oath you took to work together whenever there's a threat to our thing."

"Is it this guy? Mack?" the skater/punk bully

demanded, jerking a thumb at the golem, who was at that moment pulling a small twig out of his nose.

"No, the gol— I mean, Mack, is cool. He's on our side. In fact, he's the one in danger."

"In danger?" Popular Mean Girls bully Jennifer Schwarz asked. "Why should we care?"

Camaro thumped her on the head for that and explained, "You want someone else bullying our kids? Some outsiders who aren't even part of our thing? Think before you say something stupid."

"No way," Ed said, anxious for any chance to prove himself. "No way some outside bullies bully our victims."

"We call them clients, not victims," Camaro corrected him patiently. "Now, listen up. You see those short, stocky dudes with the long skinny fingers and the sharp teeth trying to pass themselves off as kids?"

The bullies all looked.

"Now, do you see the skinny ones with kind of buggy heads dressed in raincoats and evening dresses?"

Most of them didn't know what an evening dress was—and no surprise; it's a totally inappropriate clothing choice for a chaperone—but they were able to spot the suspicious ones nevertheless.

"There are too many for us to take them on all at once. We need to peel them off, a few at a time," Camaro said. She tilted her head and looked at the golem. Then back at the treasonous Tong Elves and the Skirrit. No, she didn't know that was what they were, but she looked at them anyway and saw again that they were totally fixated on the golem.

"We use the gol—er, Mack—as bait," Camaro said. She beckoned the golem and whispered in his ear. "I want you to walk toward the boys' room. Then, at the last minute, just as you reach the bathroom, you'll be close to the outside door, right?"

The golem had no idea if this was right. So he said, "Right."

"When you get there, do something to attract attention. Then run outside real quick!"

Camaro did not specify exactly what the golem should do to attract attention, and this would prove to be a mistake. Because the golem followed her instructions perfectly. He walked toward the boys' room. And there, just before he would have to go in, he attracted attention by sticking his tongue out.

Fourteen feet.

Golem bodies are capable of amazing things, what with basically being mud thinly disguised to look like skin and hair and clothing and so on.

So the golem didn't really have a tongue like normal people; he had as much tongue as he wanted to have. In fact he could turn much of his body into tongue, and that's what he did: first he stuck out his tongue, and then with both hands he pulled more and more tongue out until it was sort of like a limp fire hose just piling up in a coil on the floor as his body got smaller and smaller and—

And then there was a bunch of screaming as kids noticed. Some of that screaming came from Jennifer Schwarz, but pretty soon everyone—regardless of gender, race, creed, or national origin—was screaming.

It certainly did attract the attention of the Tong Elves and the Skirrit.

The golem bolted for the exit. But he was unable to move quickly due to the fact that he was dragging fourteen feet of tongue using legs now no bigger than turkey drumsticks.

"Oooookay," Camaro said, somewhat discouraged. "Let's get 'em!"

She charged at the Tong Elves, who were charging at the golem, who was dragging his tongue out into the common area outside the all-purpose room. Most of her bullies followed her, but none was exactly leading the charge.

So Camaro plowed into the back of a Tong Elf. It was like hitting a statue. Tong Elves are tough. Camaro couldn't know this—indeed, few people do—but Tong Elves are raised from the age of three in deep underground caves[26] where they are required to carve their own living space out of solid bedrock using nothing but a lighter and a hatchet. Their only drink is the condensation on cave walls, and they scrape the lichen from rocks with their specially adapted lower teeth. The lederhosen they wear are the tanned pelts of bears that they kill and skin in unarmed combat.

So, they're tough, the Tong Elves. Even the treasonous ones.

Camaro literally bounced off the Tong Elf she'd hit. But she landed well and rolled back to her feet.

---

26 A large percentage of caves are underground.

The Tong Elf turned wicked eyes on her and reached for the trident dagger that was the specialized weapon of his tong (Live Oak Tong). The weapon had three blades, the center one longer than the other two and serpentine in style.

"You filthy bag of seething worms!" the Tong Elf snarled.

"Who are you calling a . . . whatever you said?" Camaro demanded.

The Tong Elf slashed at Camaro and she dodged out of the way, but it was a close call. One of the smaller blades shaved a strand of dark hair from her head.

"Whoa!" Camaro cried.

"I'll carve you like a Thanksgiving turkey, you vile, hideous, pestilential primate!"

Camaro had been a bully since second grade, but no one had ever almost killed her. This was a new experience and she didn't like it. Her eyes darted to the wall, to the red steel-and-glass box that held the fire extinguisher. She leaped, grabbed it, and swung the heavy cylinder blindly just as the Tong Elf stabbed his three-way blade at her.

The steel cylinder caught the blades and broke one.

She raised the fire extinguisher and slammed it hard at the Tong Elf's wrinkled-up apple-doll face.

Wham!

The Tong Elf recoiled, staggered back, and Camaro was on him in a flash. She hit the Tong Elf a second, powerful blow and—

Suddenly she fell to her knees.

She dropped the fire extinguisher.

She stared down at the long, glittering steel shaft that extended out of her chest. It was smeared with blood.

Feeling stupid, she turned to see the Skirrit standing behind her, its insect claw wrapped tightly around the short spear.

The golem tried to cry out in fear, seeing Camaro fall, but his tongue first had to be raveled back into his mouth, and his body first had to reassume some kind of normal proportions, and only then could he cry, "Camaro!"

The golem ran to her and knelt beside her as the Skirrit, showing no emotion on its dead-eyed face, pulled the spear from her body.

"Golem . . . ," Camaro gasped.

"Camaro!" the golem cried.

Fighting, which had broken out between the foul creatures and the bullies, ended abruptly. It ended with half the bullies unconscious and the rest running for home and trying to come up with stories to explain why they had run in terror from their first real fight.

"Golem," Camaro said, wheezing through her pain, "they're going to try and make you do things . . . bad things. You can't let them."

"But . . . but I am just a golem," he said. "I can only be what I'm made to be."

"No, Golem," Camaro said. She grasped his arm and pulled him down to her.

The golem saw her eyes flutter and she sagged back. He howled in pain and sadness, and he twisted one of his fingers off his hand and pushed the claylike mud into her terrible wound.

"You'll be okay," he said through tears that cut small channels in his cheeks. "You have to be okay!"

"Oh, isn't this sweet?"

The golem had heard the voice before. A girl's voice, though in truth the "girl" was millennia old.

He lay Camaro's head gently on the ground, and

turned to face what he knew would be his own doom.

She was stunning, of course, her red hair blowing in a slight breeze, her lips redder still, her skin the color of cream, her eyes like green fire.

Risky.

"Come here, little golem," Risky said, and crooked her finger and smiled her crafty, evil smile. "We tried this once before and your little friend here got in the way. This time it doesn't look like she'll be much trouble."

The golem felt something then. He felt something he had never really felt before. It was like there was a fire burning inside him. It wasn't a feeling borrowed from Mack; it came from someplace else.

He leaped to his feet. His face twisted into a terrible mask of anger. And he stretched his hands out to wring Risky's neck.

"Oh, how cute," Risky said. "It has a temper."

The golem wrapped its fingers around her throat and drew her close. And that was when Risky's hand shot out like a piston and her fist rammed right into the golem's mouth.

In seconds the golem began to feel . . . strange.

Different.

He was no longer choking the evil goddess. His hands fell away from her neck and hung by his sides.

From the distance came the sound of an ambulance siren.

But here on the quad, on the grass in front of the multipurpose room, every eye—human and not human—was watching the golem.

Watching as the creature most had thought was Mack, and some knew was only a version of Mack, changed.

His skin grew gray and hard. It was as if a suit of armor was growing over him.

At the same time he was getting taller and broader, with bunches of muscles like pythons, with fingers that ended in bird-of-prey talons.

His face was the last to change. He'd looked like Mack, of course, albeit a somewhat sloppy, slightly muddy, occasionally twig-poking version of Mack.

But now his cheeks became hard slabs of steel. His mouth was a slit lined with red-rimmed steel teeth. Two horns grew from his temples—twisted, bony horns that arced forward and came to sharp points just to the side of his eyes.

"Much better," Risky purred. "Now, my little Destroyer, follow me."

She turned, laughed in delight, and walked away as the lumbering monster who had sort of been Mack followed behind her like a sullen and dangerous dog.

Seven

The Golden Temple is really, actually, gold. It's covered in gold, not gold paint. Gold gold. It's rectangular, and sits surrounded by water in an artificial lake. All around the lake are ornate, impressive white buildings that are part of the whole temple complex, but the thing that draws your attention is definitely the temple itself.

Because it's gold.

It looks like the jewelry box a queen or empress might own. Like maybe you could sort of pry the top off and it would be full of bracelets and earrings and rings.

There's a narrow, covered causeway leading out across the water to the temple. Music is playing over loudspeakers. It's not great music, really, but hey, it's music. And people from all over the world sort of shuffle down the causeway to get a look inside the temple.

There is a strict no-cuts rule, but Mack dealt with the line by showing up on a dragon. It's amazing the effect a turquoise dragon will have on people waiting in line. Fortunately the water in the lake is shallow, so the panicked worshippers and assorted tourists were in no danger of drowning as they leaped shrieking off the causeway.

Xiao landed, and Mack and Stefan dismounted at the end of the causeway, which was now almost completely clear.

"Shall I change back?" Xiao asked.

"Probably yes. I'm not sure how they feel about dragons in their temple."

The three of them—Mack, Stefan, and Xiao—walked quickly to the entrance of the temple. An old man in a bright-yellow turban stepped out to block their path. He didn't look happy about it, and in fact he was trembling a bit, but since he had a fantastic, very-nearly-impossible white beard, Mack was also trembling.

"You . . . you . . . you . . . ," the man said.

"Uh-uh-uh-uhuhuhuhuh!" Mack said.

"Move aside, old dude," Stefan said threateningly.

Fortunately Xiao was there and had the presence of mind to ask the old man what he wanted. It turned out all he wanted was for them to take off their shoes and cover their heads. With a palsied hand he offered them scarves for that last part.

It's one thing to go busting into temples with a bully and a dragon, but at the very least you have to observe the customs. So it was barefoot and scarf-headed that the three of them stepped into the Golden Temple of Amritsar.

Which was also mostly golden inside. But not just gold like someone had spray-painted a garage or whatever. No, this was gold that had been hammered on, gold on top of more gold, gold designs against gold backgrounds. Part of the ceiling had a shallow, scallop-shaped dome that was encrusted with gold and from which hung a massive chandelier made of, you guessed it . . . crystal.[27]

There was also a sort of awning set up inside where Mack assumed holy people sat and said holy things. But there was no one there at the moment. Apparently it was not a 24/7 service.

There was also an open second level, also gold, with a gold railing, a gold . . . Well, okay, you get the point: gold.

But one thing was clear: Valin was nowhere to be seen.

"I thought there were going to be lentils," Stefan said, disappointed.

"Valin came here," Mack mused. "Why? Why here?"

"I will question the old gentleman," Xiao said. "He's fleeing, but he's fleeing slowly."

It was true. The old man was fleeing very slowly, and Xiao easily caught up with him. She was back seconds later—just after Mack stopped Stefan from prying a gold flower off the wall—with the news that a very strange boy with a sword, and a man all in green,

---

27 Ha! Fooled you. You thought it would be gold.

had indeed entered the temple.

"The man says they spoke some words of a language he did not know and disappeared," Xiao reported.

The man with the amazing white beard had nerved himself to come back after Xiao reassured him. And now he pointed helpfully to a spot. There was nothing very interesting about this spot except, obviously, it was in the Golden Temple. But the spot itself wasn't different from a thousand other spots. Except for the ceiling fan.

Yes, there are ceiling fans in the Golden Temple, and yes, they are gold. In this case, though, probably just gold paint.

Mack stared up thoughtfully at the fan, which was turning slowly. Xiao and Stefan stood beside him, likewise staring thoughtfully up at the fan. Although Stefan's precise thought was, So where's the lentils?

Here's the thing to know: the people who worship at the temple are not exactly the same as the people who built the temple. The Golden Temple was started in the sixteenth century, and back in those days people knew that you couldn't just build a golden temple in the middle of a sacred lake without causing some disturbances in the space-time continuum. Of course in those ancient times they didn't call it the space-time continuum because that concept wasn't invented until *Star Trek* in the twentieth century. But those ancient builders knew some things. They knew there was something strange and compelling and magical about this spot, which back then was actually in the middle of a forest, not a city.

In fact, when they were first building the temple, they hoped to keep that strange force under control with four walls and four entrances and a lot of stone, marble, jewels, and gold.

It worked. For four centuries it worked.

Then, modern folk decided they needed some comfort. So they added ceiling fans. Had they just put in air-conditioning, that would have been fine. But a ceiling fan? That's a vortex, my friends, and vortices[28] are known disturbers of the space-time continuum.

Especially if you add Vargran.

"What words did Valin speak?" Mack mused.

"We may never know," Xiao said.

"What are lentils anyway?" Stefan wondered.

---

28 Plural of *vortex*. In case you ever need to know.

"Wait," Mack said, and snapped his fingers. And then his cell phone chimed to let him know that he had a voice mail, and worshippers and tourists alike, who had begun to filter back in, shushed him and gave him some hard stares, so he muted the phone, thus continuing to doom Richard Gere Middle School.[29]

"What if we tried . . ." And then Mack said, "*Unt-ma nos Vargran!*"

Unt-ma being the "or else" tense of the verb *repeat*. And *nos* meaning "earlier."

Suddenly the breeze blowing off the fan was a lot stiffer.

A *lot* stiffer. Like a tornado. A small but powerful vortex that just wrapped itself around Mack, Stefan, and Xiao.

Their hair whipped into their eyes. Their clothing snapped and pressed against them. They had to shout like reporters in a hurricane to be heard. The cloths they'd worn on their heads were torn away and it suddenly occurred to Mack that, whatever was happening here, it probably would have been a good idea to be wearing shoes.

---

29 Go, Fighting Pupfish!

He had tender feet, Mack did.

A fiery line, like molten gold, formed a circle around them on the floor. Mack exchanged a look with the turbanned gentleman, who nodded as if to say, "Yep, that's what happened with the other two."

And suddenly the Golden Temple was gone. Or to be more accurate, Mack, Stefan, and Xiao were no longer standing in a stiff downdraft in the temple, but were instead standing in ankle-deep water in a lake surrounded by a forest.

It wasn't much of a lake, really. If it was all as shallow as the part they were standing in, it would be easy enough to walk to the shore in any direction. And a bewildered Mack was trying to figure out just which shore would be closest when Stefan said, "Huh."

Stefan had many variations on "Huh." This particular version meant something like, "Dude, you better look at this."

Mack followed the direction of Stefan's stare. And there, on the shore behind them, were about a dozen men on horses. They were rather fantastically costumed (the men, not the horses). Some wore white robes; some looked like they were wearing animal skins; others wore what appeared to be colorful silk.

They had an amazing variety of headgear: tall fur hats that looked like they came from mountain goats, blue turbans, golden scarves, and floppy felt caps. They had amazing sashes, scarves, pennants, and belts.

None were bearded, but almost all had impressive mustaches. They were dark-skinned, similar to Valin, but with faces that wore scars that were clearly from having come too close to bladed weapons. They had bright, alert, slightly crazy eyes.

All of them were armed with a museum's worth of daggers, spears, lances, and swords in scabbards that ranged from simple oxhide to bejeweled masterpieces of the scabbarding art.

Their horses were big, shaggy beasts, often also festooned and bejeweled and spangled. The horses, too, had bright, alert, slightly crazy eyes.

"Those boys," Stefan said, offering his professional appraisal, "are trouble."

Almost lost within the scary crew was a reed-thin old man all in green. But you couldn't overlook the person clearly in charge, out in front astride the finest horse: Valin.

Valin looked like he was born on a horse. Maybe he was.

"Welcome, Mack!" Valin cried.

Then Valin drew his sword and yelled an order. The order he yelled was, "Seize them!"

Eight

This next part is a bit disturbing. If you are squeamish, maybe you should just skip this chapter. We're about to learn, finally, why Valin hated Mack and what the big issue was between them. And it involves some mild violence, but worse, young love. And worse still, a clown.

But we're not quite there yet. First we have a sudden charge by a dozen armed horsemen brandishing swords and pointing spears. The speed of the attack was such that Xiao hesitated between casting a Vargran spell and changing back to dragon and ended up doing nothing but emitting a frustrated "Oh!" before spears were all up in their faces.

"I have you now!" Valin cried. Then, looking disappointed, he said, "Where is my half sister? Where is Sylvie?"

"Okay, Valin, it's time to have this out!" Mack said.

"Indeed it is! Men: if the girl begins to change, stick a spear in her. And look out for the blond one: he's dangerous."

Stefan was very pleased to be described as dangerous. Although even he was feeling less than formidable with a spear point pressing into his back and a sword blade at his throat.

"Yemak, Ivan, Stenka, bind them tightly and watch them closely, spears at their throats at all times," Valin ordered. He was totally in charge. Then as the horsemen were tying Xiao and Stefan, Valin cautioned, "Don't any of you fools get drunk. The man who allows them to escape will deal with my Brembles."

At this point Mack had no idea what a Bremble was, but he saw the very respectful looks on the faces of these tough guys, and that convinced him that

Brembles were not something to be taken lightly.

Mack was snatched up by powerful hands and settled onto the saddle of a horse. A rough rope went around his wrists, a rag was stuffed in his mouth, and suddenly he was racing through the woods as thin branches whipped his face. It was all very exciting in a way. The hoofbeats were a dull thunder; the landscape flashed by; the saddle pounded his butt; a chill breeze froze his wet, bare feet.

Exciting, uncomfortable, and scary. Three things that often go together.

Paddy "Nine Iron" Trout looked extremely uncomfortable. Horseback riding can jar your bones and bruise your butt, and Nine Iron had very old bones and a meatless butt. Also, frankly, he looked ridiculous on a horse.

It occurred to Mack that this would be a good time to lay on some Vargran, if he could get the rag out of his mouth. But he was trying to figure Valin out, trying to bring him over to the side of good and truth and justice and all of that stuff, not destroy him. He needed Valin. The whole world needed Valin.

They rode for an hour through sparse forest and

across a number of shallow streams. At last they came upon a circle of tents. The tents were not colorful nylon or even dull canvas. They were large, round, lumpy things made of some kind of skin. Mack hoped it was cowhides and not human skin. Because that would have been disturbing.

One tent was larger than the rest, and Valin, with six of the big, hairy guys, marched Mack, Xiao, and Stefan into that tent.

It smelled of fire, burned meat, and sweat. That last element was supplied by a very large man with a very large mustache. He was naked to the waist and chewing on what might have been a leg of lamb.

Valin spoke some words to the man and pushed Mack to his knees.

"This is Taras Bulba," Valin said to Mack. "He's an up-and-comer with the Cossacks."

"Mhhrr hmm hnn hnh," Mack said. Because he still had a rag in his mouth.

Valin drew his dagger and placed it against Mack's neck. "One word of Vargran and I cut your throat." He pulled the rag from Mack's mouth.

"Pleased to meet you, Mr. Blubba."

"Bulba," Valin hissed. "Taras Bulba. He and his Cossacks are here to participate in the coming battle between Mukhlis Khan and Guru Hargobind."

Mack frowned. This felt like the kind of thing that might be on the test. And already he'd forgotten all the names.

"Battle?" he said.

"Yeah, Mughals and Sikhs. With a little help from the Cossacks."

Taras Bulba seemed to catch the general drift of what was being discussed and he liked battle talk. He drew an amazing scimitar with his free hand and brandished both it and the leg of lamb while yelling something enthusiastic in a language Mack had no chance of ever understanding.

"Taras Bulba was down here guarding a group of Cossack traders, and now it looks like he might get dragged into this war, since the guru's men confiscated his trade goods."

"What does any of this have to do with . . ." Mack stopped talking and began noticing certain things. For example, he noticed that all of the men in the room, like the men on horses, carried swords. And the tent was made of skins. And there was an open fire.

And he noticed that no one was on a smartphone. No one. When was the last time you saw a dozen people in a skin tent and no one was texting?

Then Mack noticed a person he'd missed at first. She was about his age. She had black hair down to her waist and was dressed in a long robe-like thing. Mack was not a fashion expert. It probably had some better name, but "robe-like thing" was all he could manage.

She was a beautiful girl. She had almond-shaped eyes and a tiny nose and high cheekbones, and her only possible beauty flaw was the fact that she had a noticeable underbite. In other words, her jaw stuck out just a bit too far.

This girl was also not texting. Nor did she have earbuds in.

She was looking hard at Mack.

Mack said, "OMG?"

No flicker of recognition in the girl's eyes.

"BRB?" he said, testing her.

Nothing.

There was only one possible explanation, and it took Mack's breath away. "What year is this?"

Valin laughed. "Very good, Mack. You aren't stupid, I'll say that. You have guessed right: this is not the twenty-first century. We have traveled back in time. This is the year 1634."

Mack blinked. "What?"

"The year 1634. Where—when, I should say—you will witness the betrayal, the terrible humiliation visited on my family by yours. Do you see that girl?"

"The one with the underbite?"

"That's not fair!" Valin cried. "They didn't have orthodontists yet!"

The outburst drew the attention of Taras Bulba. He smelled trouble, and he liked trouble. Also leg of lamb.

"You dare to insult her?" Valin demanded.

"I didn't mean to I was just—"

"That is Boguslawa Bulba, my great-great-great-great-great—"

"Can we just—"

"Silence! You made me lose count! She is my great-great-great-great-great-great-great . . . How many is that?"

"Seven."

"Okay, nine more. Sixteen greats in all. Grand-mother."

Just then the tent flap opened and in walked a good-looking lad in breeches and a sheepskin jacket. He had skin as pale as milk, freckles, and curly brown hair.

Something about the curly brown hair seemed familiar to Mack. He felt as if he'd seen it somewhere before.

Like . . . in the mirror.

"And that is your great-great-great-etc.-grandfather," Valin said poisonously. "Sean Patrick O'Flanagan MacAvoy!"

Taras Bulba spotted the young Irish boy and smiled. He waved him over and gave an affectionate rub to his hair. This had the useful side effect of cleaning some of the leg-o'-lamb grease from Bulba's hands.

"What's he doing here?" Mack asked.

"They're engaged," Valin said. "Your great-great-great-etc.-grandfather is engaged to marry my great-great-great-etc.-grandmother. But in two days he's going to dump her. She will be so humiliated that she runs away and joins a group of traveling troubadours, jugglers, and actors. This will infuriate Taras Bulba, who will disown Boguslawa. She will end up marrying not Sean Patrick, whose own descendants will be famous warriors and distillers, but a mere performer. And thus will sixteen generations of my family be raised not as descendants of the famous Taras Bulba, Cossack royalty, but rather as the descendants of a random Cossack girl and . . . Izmir. Izmir the Clown."

"Wait," Mack said. "That's the reason you're trying to kill me and doom the entire human race to subjugation by the Pale Queen? Because some ancestor of mine dumped some ancestor of yours?"

"You make it sound trivial," Valin said. "Sixteen generations of humiliation all caused by your family! But I should be Cossack royalty! I could have been a prince!"

MEANWHILE, MUCH, MUCH FURTHER BACK IN TIME

The grand opening of the Babylon temple of the Pale Queen was finally at hand. It was a gala day. Which was fine because a gal a day was about all Gil Gamesh could handle, especially when the gal in question was, shall we say, difficult.

"Did you check everything?" Risky demanded. She strode nervously up and down the main aisle of the temple, wringing her hands. "How about the blood gutter? Did you check the slope of the blood gutter? It's really important: too steep and the blood flows by so fast we can't really enjoy it."

"Yes, yes, for like the tenth time, Risky, I checked the blood gutter. I tested it out. It worked great."

She spun on her heel, which made her red hair flare out and caused his heart to skip a beat as it always did. "Did you test it with blood or water? Because the viscosity is totally different."

Risky had figured this out centuries before Isaac Newton even started thinking about it. She was evil, but she was not dumb.

Gil listened patiently to this odd fantasy of Risky's—he thought she often pretended to know things that were patently untrue. Just the other day she had talked about going around the world. Like you could go around a square dinner plate perched on the rear end of Marduk's donkey. I mean, as if.

But even as Gil tried to be patient, Risky's haranguing tone was grinding his last nerve. It had not been easy getting this temple built. Even simple things like measuring a slab of stone could be very difficult—the invention of the tape measure was still thousands of years in the future. They would measure in "feet," but each foot was slightly different, and after a man's foot had been cut off, it would shrivel up and the toes would curl, so that a "foot" measured with a fresh foot would be different from one measured with a more stale foot.

And with the invention of basic math still far in the future as well, no one could add beyond ten. The temple ended up having to be ten tens of ten feet. Of course in modern times we'd know this was a thousand feet, but back in those days, that would have meant a thousand people hobbling along on just one foot. Or five hundred people crawling without both feet, but that's getting into multiplication and division, and believe me, Gil and the Babylonians were not up for that yet.

Hardest of all was the massive statue of the Pale Queen that would dominate the altar. And that was Gil's special, personal responsibility.

Gil had assembled the finest sculptors from all

over Babylon and the nearby kingdoms of Ur of the Chaldees, Um of the Chaldees, Mill Valley, and Hork-Bajir. But since the Pale Queen would not sit for them, they had to operate on Risky's description of her. Risky was not good with descriptions and offered only that her mother was a controlling witch who never let Risky have any fun. As a result, the statue, which stood two hundred hands high (don't even ask), looked a bit like Pikachu (who also would not be invented for thousands of years) but with white hair and a gown made of the tears of children. But Gil thought he'd managed the whole thing pretty well. Probably. And anyway, the Pale Queen would surely be understanding.

Right? he asked himself nervously. Right?

Risky had not seen the final product. It was covered with a cloth—a very big cloth—and awaited the unveiling before the Pale Queen herself.

Now the great day was at last at hand. A thousand sacrificial animals had been stocked in the fenced enclosure outside. Pigs, cows, sheep, unicorns,[30] baboons, auks, rocs, hipsters, hippos, and ducks all waited to be

---

30 The idea of "endangered species" hadn't really caught on yet.

ritually slaughtered for the glory of the Pale Queen.

If that seems harsh, bear in mind that it had taken all of Gil's influence to keep humans out of it, and the truth was, even then, there were a few unfortunates who'd wandered too close and been reclassified as "goats" in order to round out the numbers.

Gil gave Risky a hug. "Don't worry, sweetheart, your mother will love it."

"I hope so. Because if she doesn't, she'll eat you," Risky said, giving him a little peck on the cheek.

"Say what now?" Gil asked.

"And did you finish the story you'll be reading to her?"

"The epic?" Gil sighed. "I only hope it lives up to its name. I'm afraid there are some plot holes."

"Try to clean those up. Mother is a stickler for plots that make sense."

"Ah. And if she . . ."

"Yes, my love, she'll probably eat you. In fact, there's a pretty good chance that even if everything goes perfectly, she'll eat you."

This was news to Gil, who was not happy. "Shouldn't you have warned me about this?"

Risky made a pouty face and stabbed an angry finger at the murals that lined the walls. Each of them showed the Pale Queen in one fabulous outfit or another eating various legendary and historical figures: Adam, Eve, Zoroaster, Dagan, Astarte, Noah, and various pharaohs. "It's like you didn't even pay attention to your own artwork!"

"I didn't think it was literal. I thought it was more metaphorical. I thought eating people symbolized, I don't know, the state of a corrupt society."

"No, she eats people."

"Some family you have," Gil snapped.

"Oh, do not go there," Risky said, waving a scolding finger in his face. "Do not dis my family."

"Let's not squabble," Gil said. He tried out his most winning smile, but the truth was, he was feeling a little sick to his stomach. What if it was his own blood in the blood gutter? Would that be irony?[31] He had a lot of plans for the future, and none of them involved being chewed on by a malevolent, demonic goddess.

"Hey, look at the time!" he said, glancing at his wrist only to discover that watches had not been invented

---

31 Yes.

yet. "I, uh . . . There are some things . . . Hmm, I have a thing to do. Some, uh . . . writing. Yeah."

"Is it a love poem?"

"What? Yeah, that's right. You guessed it! I was going to write you a love poem. Aww, now you ruined the surprise, but I'm still going to write you, like, a fantastic poem."

"Then get to it, silly," Risky said.

Gil exited the temple with the intention of writing a poem, all right, but not a love poem. And also he would be writing it a long, long way from Babylon.

He raced to the holding pen full of sacrificial animals and yelled, "Are there any horses here?"

One of the humans reclassified as sacrificial "goats" said, "If it means getting out of here, I can pretend to be a horse!"

Which was how Gil Gamesh ended up riding for his life from Babylon on the back of a cheesemaker's curd-skimmer slave named Enkidu.

They rested for a moment atop a nearby hill and looked back just in time to see a massive pillar of oily smoke rising from the desert on the other side of the city. Inside that greasy black smoke was a fell beast of incredible size—the world's sole surviving apatosaurus. It walked with a slow, shambling gait. Atop that apatosaurus on a slightly unsteady canopied saddle rode the Pale Queen. An army of monsters walked before her and behind her.

"Okay," Enkidu said brightly after seeing what was coming. "I've rested plenty!"

"Let's get out of here," Gil agreed.

Nine

Valin's plan was obvious: he clearly wanted Mack to find some way to rewrite history. He would hold Stefan's and Xiao's lives hostage to ensure that Mack did not flee.

Mack definitely would have fled if given half a chance. For one thing, the Cossacks struck him as a bunch of guys who would just as soon cut your head off as say hello. In fact they were so heavily armed all the time that if you happened to just accidentally bump into one, you were in danger of losing a hand.

The other reason Mack wanted out was that he didn't think it was a good idea to mess with time travel. Who knew what damage he might do? What if he did manage to convince Sean Patrick O'Flanagan MacAvoy to continue seeing Boguslawa? What if they got married? What if they had kids? What if those kids became evil and altered the course of history? Or for that matter, what if they were great and amazing geniuses who invented cars way too early?

On the other hand, obviously whatever he did couldn't change the future too much, could it? After all, if he changed the future so much that he himself was not born, then he wouldn't have existed to come back in time and cause himself not to be born. Would he?

These kinds of thoughts brought on headaches, and when he explained them to his friends, they were no help.

Xiao, who was constantly guarded by two Cossack warriors, simply said, "These things are unknowable. You must do what you feel in your heart is right."

And Stefan, who was guarded by nine Cossack warriors, said, "Huh," which in this case meant, "I don't like paradoxes." And he would threaten to punch

Mack if Mack insisted on trying to talk metaphysics.[32]

Mack missed Sylvie. She totally would have talked about paradoxes with him.

Mack decided to focus on simply getting himself and his friends out of trouble. The easy way seemed to be to convince Sean Patrick O'Flanagan MacAvoy to remain true to Boguslawa.

All he had to do was change the future in such a way that Valin did not become the descendant of someone named Izmir the Clown.

So . . . change the future, but without changing the future.

Headache pills were still hundreds of years away from being invented, so Mack shrugged it off, said, "Whatever," and at the first opportunity introduced himself to Sean Patrick O'Flanagan MacAvoy.

"Hey, my name's Mack."

It was a couple of days after Mack had been rudely shanghaied to the seventeenth century, and they were watching a game of polo. Polo is a game where men on horses hit a ball using long-handled hammers. In

---

32 Metaphysics: a branch of philosophy concerned with the fundamental nature of reality. Lay that word on your teacher someday. Your teacher will call your parents in and tell them you're a genius.

Cossack polo the ball was a head. Yes, they were a pretty tough bunch of guys, the Cossacks.

"*Cad ba mhaith leat*?" Sean Patrick replied. Because he was Irish and spoke only Irish, and just enough Russian to converse with his Cossack girlfriend.

Mack was reluctant to use up any of his *enlightened puissance*—after all, anything might happen—but he had no choice, so he used a Vargran spell that allowed him to understand what Sean Patrick was saying, and to be understood in return.

It turned out all Sean Patrick had said was, "What do you want?"

"Oh, um, just . . . hi."

"Hello, fellow."

"So. Your girlfriend. She's hot, huh?" This was an amazingly stupid thing to say, and Mack was relieved that the Cossacks standing around didn't stab him right then and there. This was, after all, the daughter of Taras Bulba he was calling "hot."

"She should step outside if she's hot," Sean Patrick said. "It's chilly outside."

Having dodged that bullet, Mack wondered how

to proceed. "So. Um. You two are tight, right? I mean, you're totally going to marry Boguslawa. Right?"

Sean Patrick stuck his thumbs in his belt and puffed out his chest and said, "I have pledged my undying love."

"Good. And nothing could possibly change that, right?"

"Why? What have you heard?"

There was a loud roar of approval as out on the polo field one of the Cossacks swung his mallet and sent the battered head-ball flying. The horses thundered toward the goal.

So far this was going badly for Mack. But things were about to go much worse. Because not all those thundering hooves were from Cossack polo ponies. There was a host of horsemen rushing from the south, and judging by the beards and turbans, they were not Cossacks.

Suddenly arrows were sprouting in the chests of Cossack polo players. Which is a poetic way of saying that they were getting killed by bows and arrows from the attacking army.

Valin rushed to Mack, grabbed his arm, and

hissed, "We have to get out of here! Sean Patrick, get Boguslawa!"

But Sean Patrick was already beating feet toward the distant woods. An arrow passed so close to Boguslawa that the feathers smeared her lipstick.

"Ah!" Mack cried. He grabbed Boguslawa's hand and yelled to Xiao and Stefan, "Let's get out of here!"

Their Cossack guards had bigger problems than chasing them right then, so the four of them—a boy-hero and his bully-bodyguard from twenty-first-century Sedona and a dragon-girl from twenty-first-century China and a Cossack princess-babe from seventeenth-century Russia—all ran into the Punjabi woods just ahead of a guru-general's army.

It was all very confusing, but when there are arrows and spears flying, it's pretty easy to focus on fleeing.

Ten

Here's what was going on. Mukhlis Khan was invading India and Guru Hargobind was trying to stop him. Taras Bulba was just there to see if he could get a job working for one side or the other. He was your average, hardworking savage warlord and he needed a job.

Valin was there helping Taras Bulba and trying to rewrite history.

Paddy "Nine Iron" Trout was there trying to get Valin to kill Mack.

None of this will be on the test. Just understand

this: Valin would never join the Magnificent Twelve so long as he blamed Mack for being descended from Izmir the Clown.

Okay, that didn't really explain much. One more try.

Mack, Xiao, Stefan, and some girl named Boguslawa were in the woods, scared, damp, and shoeless. No one knew what had happened to Valin.

Oh, and here's where things go really bad:

Boguslawa, panting, breathless, her black hair blowing in the breeze, threw her arms around Mack's neck and said, "Вы спасли мне жизнь!"

Which, translated, means, "You saved my life!"

And then she kissed Mack on both cheeks.

Stefan and Xiao both stared.

"I weel not marry Sean Patrick MacAvoy," Boguslawa said breathlessly. "He is run away. I weel marry you. My hero!"

"Huh," Stefan said, meaning, "Uh-oh."

"What. Wait. What?" Mack squeaked. "No. Wait."

"I am wanting man who is strong and brave," Boguslawa insisted. "Not frighten lady-boy Sean Patrick, run away poof!"

They could have discussed it in more detail but they heard pounding hooves and deep, manly shouts, and there was no way to know if they were good guys or bad guys. For that matter, how did they even know which side were the good guys?

So they ran. Twigs and thorns tore at Mack's unprotected feet, but that was better than waiting around to get a sword stuck in him.

To Xiao, Mack said, "Can you carry the three of us?"

"I don't think so," she said. "But I can probably scare off our pursuers."

Sure enough, she transformed into her real self and slithered neatly through the trees. Within a few minutes Mack heard confused shouts of terror and the loud whinnying of scared horses. Xiao, in human form again, came back more slowly, leading two horses.

To keep the weight balanced equally on the horses, they put their largest person (Stefan) and their smallest person (Xiao) together on one horse while Mack and Boguslawa shared the other.

Which meant Boguslawa riding with her arms around Mack's waist and her head resting on his shoulder while he desperately considered how he was going to get out of this mess.

At least Valin wasn't with them, and with any luck at all, he would never see them.

They kept on through the woods with no real idea where they were going, and Mack was beginning to despair. "We have to get back to our own time. The Pale Queen is coming and we're, like, four hundred years away from it. Besides, I don't want to live in the seventeenth century. We have a job to do. We're supposed to save the world—four hundred years from now!"

"I never even got any lentils," Stefan said.

"There may be food in the saddlebags," Xiao suggested.

So they looked. Some sort of jerky and . . . yes, lentils!

"That's lentils?" Stefan asked, disappointed. "Huh."

"Listen, Boguslawa, you have to marry Sean Patrick." Mack really wished he had shoes while giving an impassioned speech from horseback. He half turned in the saddle so she could see his face. "The fate of the world depends on it. If you don't marry Sean Patrick, all that is good and decent will die."

"I am marry you, Meck. Sean Patrick he is baby crying and run away. Meck is brave like lion."

"Wait. What if . . . What if it was Sean Patrick who was brave and I was a coward?"

Boguslawa shrugged. "I am daughter of Taras Bulba. I must marry brave man, not coward."

Mack sighed. "We have to find Valin and Sean Patrick."

Xiao shook her head. "If we find Sean Patrick, we will find Valin, too, I believe."

And so they rode off toward the east, not realizing that was the wrong way. They really had no idea where they were going. But there was no one to ask directions of, and horses just do not come with a built-in navigation system.

Mack even tried the maps app on his phone. He knew it wouldn't work, but it comforted him somehow to have this shiny object from the future as a reminder.

Then he saw that he'd had a call. And a voice mail. Both from the golem. Sadly the message could not be played because, well, pretty much every single thing that would make voice mail possible didn't exist yet.

It worried him. But then, he had plenty of other things to worry about. The golem would have to manage on his own.

Eleven

MEANWHILE, 7,831 MILES (AND 400 YEARS) AWAY, IN SEDONA, ARIZONA

Camaro lay dying.

But she didn't die.

Oh, she should have. The Skirrit lance had pierced her heart, and that is the kind of thing that causes death. But the bleeding had been slowed by the detached finger of the golem. It seemed to be nothing but mud; however, there's a big difference between mud mud and mud that's been fashioned into a golem and given magical life.

The golem's magic stopped the bleeding. It knit torn veins and arteries back together. It fused flesh. It melded the strands of muscle.

When Grimluk shaped the golem, he did so with mud and twigs and one more ingredient: the magic of the Vargran tongue when spoken by one who possesses the *enlightened puissance*. It was that magic that kept the golem alive and functioning and basically immortal. And now a bit of the golem was working to heal Camaro Angianelli.

Ten minutes after being fatally stabbed, Camaro took off the oxygen mask the emergency medical technicians had put on her, and ripped the needle from her arm, and stood up and said, "I really do not like that redhead."

Camaro wasn't dead, but she was definitely worn out, so she went home and had a good night's sleep.

The next morning she set out in search of "Mack," but the golem could not be found. She went to his house, knocked on the door, and asked Mack's father if he knew where Mack was.

"Hmmm," Mack's father said thoughtfully. "Is today his football practice?"

Today was not his football practice. Because Mack was not on the football team. So, obviously, neither was the golem.

Camaro didn't want to upset the MacAvoy family, so she did not tell them of her suspicion that "Mack" was about to be made the unwitting slave of an evil demon goddess. For one thing, there was no way for her to explain it without sounding jealous of Risky.

Camaro was not jealous. Though it was true that Risky was stunningly beautiful while she, Camaro, was merely cute edging toward pretty, she was not jealous.

No way. Why would she be?

She thought all this through as she walked the streets of Sedona, occasionally yelling, "Mack! Mack!" Though she wished she could call out, "Golem!"

Camaro searched everywhere, all through the neighborhoods and all up and down 89A, which was the main road through town.

Finally, dusty, hot, thirsty, and discouraged, she became far more discouraged when she ran into a woman she knew outside the run-down, sleazy, disreputable Arpaio Motel at the farthest limits of the town. Camaro bought a bottle of water and recognized the manager.

"Hey, aren't you Mrs. Lafrontiere?"

"That's me, honey." She was an older woman, if by "older," you meant "in her forties." She was drinking a cup of tea and gazing off toward the red limestone hills that surround Sedona.

"I'm looking for someone," Camaro said. "One is a kind of monsterlike thing, and the other is a redhead."

Mrs. Lafrontiere—who, like much of the population of Sedona, was also a clairvoyant spiritual healer as well as motel manager—nodded. She looked closely, suspiciously at Camaro. "I saw them. It was late last night. A frightening creature ten feet tall. And a girl with red hair. She had the most extraordinary green eyes, perfect pale skin, a wonderful body—"

"Yeah, that's them," Camaro interrupted. Frankly she'd heard enough about Risky's looks.

"She was an incomparable beauty with—"

"She's not that pretty," Camaro snapped.

"Like an angel, she was."

"Yeah, whatever. Where did they go?"

The woman pointed a heavily bejeweled hand toward the hills. "Up Schnebly Hill." She shivered then, and met Camaro's gaze. "Where else would a demon goddess and a golem go?"

Camaro pointedly ignored the reference to a golem. No one should know that, but Mrs. Lafrontiere was a clairvoyant after all. She looked up at the hill. It was quite red in the slanting rays of the sun. Many believed it was a place of special power, of mysticism, a nexus of supernatural manifestation.

It scared Camaro a bit. But worse yet, there was no way to walk that far. So sadly, reluctantly, she turned back toward town. In the end, she knew, the golem would return as the Destroyer.

"This isn't going to end well," Camaro said.

Twelve

Mack, too, was thinking, This isn't going to end well. But due to the unfortunate fact that he'd been transported four hundred years into the past, he was thinking it a long time before Camaro thought the same thing.

Also, his feet were cold.

They stumbled finally on a village. It was a primitive place, the village. The village was so primitive it didn't even have a name. At the edge of the village was a sign announcing, "Welcome to" and then just a blank space.

But it was a friendly village just the same. They offered Mack and his little troop a meal of cholera water and eels. Mack traded them the lentils for a pair of shearling-lined boots[33] sewn together with distressed-tendon string. He was glad of that, though Stefan was bitter over the lentils.

"We're looking for a guy who looks kind of like me," Mack said to the village elder.

The village elder thought about that for a minute, looked around, nodded thoughtfully, and pointed at Mack.

"No, not me. He looks like me."

The village elder once again nodded thoughtfully, then stroked his chin and pointed at Mack.

This happened six more times before Mack realized that this village was so small that it couldn't afford both a village elder and a village idiot and had therefore combined both jobs into one.[34]

Xiao and Stefan went out to look around the village in the vain hope that there had to be a store or a restaurant or something other than nine mud-and-wattle huts surrounded by trees. Mack stayed with

---

33 Yep, an early form of Uggs.

34 Today the man would be in Congress.

Boguslawa and the village elder/idiot.

"I am wanting to have nice house, many goats, and children," Boguslawa said. "Must be paint and have two windows. Also deep poop hole in floor."

"Look," Mack snapped impatiently, "you and I are not engaged. For one thing, we're twelve years old."

"Is old, yes, for engagement," Boguslawa said. "But must be engaged before can be married."

"Listen to me," Mack grated. His feet were warming up, but all that did was allow him to pay attention to the other stuff that was bothering him. "I am not your boyfriend!"

Boguslawa's face fell. Tears filled her eyes. Her lower lip began to quiver. "You are not liking me?"

Mack rolled his eyes and threw up his hands. "That's not it, Boguslawa. Look, I do like you. I like you a lot. You're beautiful and . . . and, like, sweet and all. And really, if I wasn't busy saving the world, and also twelve, I would totally marry you. But where I come from? You can't get married until you're old."

"You mean fourteen?" Boguslawa asked, aghast.

Mack thought he had hit upon a good way to put

an end to all thoughts of marriage. "Even older," he said. "I mean, hey, of course if I could, I would totally be your boyfriend but—"

Boguslawa squealed in misplaced delight and threw her arms around Mack.

"A*ha*!" Valin cried.

Because, yes, he had followed Mack through the woods and all the way to the nameless village and had snuck quietly[35] up and overheard the last of that conversation.

"Valin!" Mack cried. "It's not what it looks like!"

Valin pushed his way into the hut. Unfortunately the hut wasn't very well built and the whole thing sort of just fell over, so that now Mack and Boguslawa and the village elder/idiot were just sitting around a weak fire out in the open.

Mack saw, then, just how serious this was going to be. First, Paddy "Nine Iron" Trout was standing with his sword-cane in sword mode.

And second, there were some exceedingly large creatures with stabby razor-wire hands standing all around the village.

---

35 Sneaking is often done quietly.

"I see you've noticed my Brembles," Valin said. "Brembles! Seize him!"

Which was how Mack ended up stretched out in the sun later that day with ants stinging him to death.

See how that came full circle?

And now Mack gets stung to death.

Thirteen

From a distance—they were "shopping" at the village's only store, Fleas, Dung, and Beyond—Xiao and Stefan saw Valin and Nine Iron and the Brembles take Mack away.

Stefan started to charge in recklessly, but Xiao put a restraining hand on his arm. (She wasn't attracted to humans, being a dragon, but Stefan did have impressive biceps.)

"No," Xiao said. "This may be an opportunity."

"What?" Stefan scowled at her suspiciously. "He's under my wing!"

"You will not prevail against the Brembles. I know this species. They are mentioned in some of my father's books. Once, long ago, they troubled China and were driven off only by deploying vast armies. If you attack, you will die. And Mack along with you."

Stefan hesitated. The whole "fear" thing was foreign to him. But he understood the part about not being able to save Mack anyway. His job wasn't to act all brave, it was to actually keep Mack safe.

Boguslawa was also left behind by an angry, contemptuous Valin, who called her "a faithless strumpet." Boguslawa spotted Xiao and Stefan and made her way toward them, weeping and wailing.

"Quickly, before that annoying girl gets here. We must find Sean Patrick. It is the only way to change the course of history and unite him with Boguslawa. I will fly!"

"What? You're going to leave me with that girl?" Stefan was fearless, absolutely fearless. And yet he wasn't sounding fearless.

"Just don't let anything happen to her. The fate of the world may rest on it!" Xiao cried. Then, hesitating, she added in a whisper, "Don't be brave. You must seem to be cowardly."

"Why?"

"She admires courage. Do you want her to admire you?"

She slipped easily back into dragon form.

Boguslawa freaked out. Stefan had gotten used to seeing Xiao suddenly revealed as a Chinese dragon, but it was all new to Boguslawa. Stefan was about to tell her it was no big deal, but Xiao was right: Boguslawa seemed to have a thing for strong, fearless men. And Stefan knew what he looked like: he was a very good-looking guy. If you liked the tall, blond, icy blue eyes, chiseled features, rippling muscles type of guy.[36]

It was time for some acting. But pretending to be afraid did not come naturally to Stefan since he'd never really been afraid. However: he'd been with Mack during at least a dozen phobia meltdowns.

"Oh!" Stefan cried. "Oh that's like scary! Ah. Ah. That creeps me out when she does that."

"It was disturbing, but . . . ," Boguslawa said.

"Uh. Uh uh uh uh!" cried Stefan, getting into it a little bit. "Gagagagagagaga!"

"She is gone away, so no more gagagagaga, yes?"

"I have dragon phobia," Stefan said, having now

---

36 Girls sometimes do.

exhausted his sound effects. "It's . . . kind of rare."

Boguslawa rolled her eyes. "You are having big muscles not big heart like a lion."

"Yeah," Stefan said, feeling a bit of shame even though it was all an act. He sighed. "Let's keep riding, huh?"

And they did keep riding.

There was no way they could possibly realize that at that very moment Mack was being pinned down by Brembles.

And no way to know that Mack would panic and waste his *enlightened puissance* on disappearing some creepy beetles.

And no way to know that Valin was—at that very moment—guiding deadly red ants into a jar that he would forthwith dump on Mack's face.

Fourteen

Which brings us back to:

"Let me go!" Mack cried. He pulled at the chulks, but no, he wasn't pulling his way out of this one. The Brembles had him. Valin had him.

And the ants had him.

A second ant stung.

A third.

And now the stinging signal went out through all the ants.

Mack was about to die a most terrible death.

Really.

A fourth and fifth sting made Mack yell and thrash wildly. But now there was no more counting; the stings came fast and furious, a wave of them, pain upon pain, and already Mack felt himself swelling up, felt his airway constrict, felt his heart hammering way too fast, felt . . .

. . . felt death itself approaching, extending its bony claw to snuff the life from him.

"Hug! Ligean dó dul!"

Which obviously is Irish for, "Hey, let him go!"

Mack could barely see—that one ant was still right on his eyeball, and he was dying, after all—but across the field came Sean Patrick MacAvoy. He was armed with a sword and went charging straight at Valin.

Paddy "Nine Iron" Trout raised his cane-sword, preparing to stab Sean Patrick through the heart. Of course this was happening slowly, so unless Sean Patrick stopped to take a short nap, he wasn't in too much danger from the Nafia assassin.

But the Brembles were a different story entirely. All four of the massive, terrifying, evil (soon to be extinct) creatures drew themselves up, ready for a fight. This meant pulling their chulks from the ground, which in turn freed Mack, who was gasping for breath, swelling up, thinking seriously about vomiting, and starting to wonder why the whole world was spinning around and around and around.

The Brembles made an interesting sound. It went like this: *KIIIIILLLLLL!*

The funny thing is that Brembles don't know any actual words, so it's totally coincidental that their wordless, incoherent, oddly high-pitched shriek sounds like a drawn-out version of the word *kill*.

Then again, even though they don't know the word *kill*, that's obviously what they mean when they shriek that way and begin bounding like nightmare hyenas brandishing their chulks and the surrounding tangle of thorns and baring their six rows of teeth.[37]

Sean Patrick stopped running then because . . . well, because he was about to be killed, that's why. His face was pale as a ghost. Mack was pretty bleary but he thought he might be seeing knees actually knocking together.

"Noooooooo!" Valin cried. "Brembles! To me!"

---

37 Seven rows among the more elderly Brembles.

The Brembles didn't seem to hear; they were about three big bounces away from hitting Sean Patrick like a freight train full of pain.

"*Subze-ma Brembles!*"

Valin had used Vargran meaning "Freeze, Brembles!" And sure enough, the Brembles stopped cold. Like statues. Frozen in midslaver.

"You can't kill him! He may still be my great-great-great-great-great-great—"

Mack detected a note of impatience from the Brembles despite the fact that they were frozen.

"—great-great-great-grandfather!"

Sean Patrick, to his credit, had recovered his composure, and you almost couldn't see the spot where he had peed his breeches. He had not dropped his sword, and now he advanced with a step that was somewhere about halfway between a swagger and a mince.

"Yeah," he said, but in Irish. "Take that. You monsters! I'm not afraid of you!"

And then, though his vision was pretty sketchy, Mack was sure he saw Stefan and Xiao walking toward them. With them was Boguslawa.

Boguslawa broke into a run. Stefan started to go

after her, but Xiao held him back.

Boguslawa ran to Sean Patrick.

"You are so brave!"

"*Go raibh maith agat*," Sean Patrick said. "Thanks."

"I am now loving you," she said, and looked shyly at Sean Patrick.

"I thought you thought I was a weakling and a coward," Sean Patrick said. "That's why I was going to break up with you. I couldn't spend my life with someone who thought I was a coward."

"Of course, when you were weak, scaredy not-a-man, I was contempting you. I am daughter of great Taras Bulba! I am Cossack princess! But now you are not coward, but brave like angry buffalo! So now I am loving you."

Meanwhile, while all this was going on, Mack was dying of ant venom. In fact he wasn't entirely sure he hadn't hallucinated the whole thing. It certainly was strange enough to be a hallucination. And how was it Sean Patrick could speak English now?

Xiao knelt beside him and spoke some Vargran words that he almost didn't hear because his ears were swollen shut from the stings.

And then he was fine.

This is the excellent thing about magic as opposed to medicine: it works much faster.

"So you'll marry Boguslawa?" Valin asked.

Sean Patrick shrugged. "If she'll have me. I thought she despised me. I can't marry someone who despises me."

"I am not despising you, you are brave and handsome!" Boguslawa cried, and hugged him.

So it was happiness all over except for the fact that Sean Patrick, overcome with joy, started to say something. He started to say:

"This is wonderful. Now I can realize my dream of becoming a—"

And that's when Xiao tripped and plowed into him in such a way that she accidentally punched him in the jaw.

"So sorry!" Xiao said. "But, moving on, such a happy day!"

Valin, suddenly very formal, said, "Mack MacAvoy, this resolves the feud that has existed between our families for—"

"A feud I knew nothing about and had nothing to do with!" Mack pointed out. If by "pointed out" you mean "angrily asserted."

"I hereby declare the blood feud over!" Valin said.

"Oh no you . . . ," Paddy "Nine Iron" said, and reached for his mask.

And breathed.

And breathed.

And breathed.

"Don't!" And with that he raised his sword-cane, pointed it at Valin, and yelled, "Traitor!"

He plunged the sword into Valin's heart. In his imagination.

Put it this way: he intended to plunge the sword into Valin's heart. But between the moment when Paddy decided on that course of action and when he actually did the whole plunging thing, something like sixty seconds passed. During which time Valin had stepped out of the way, patted Paddy on the shoulder, and said, "You've been a good mentor to me. Let's not spoil it with a long good-bye."

"We need to get back to our own time," Mack said. The truth was he was feeling very cranky, very resentful, even peeved at Valin. He had a strong desire to punch the crazy kid in the stomach. But he had a job to do. There was a world to be saved, and the clock was ticking. So he swallowed hard, gritted his teeth, and said, "Are you with us, Valin?"

Valin did a sort of bow, a rather dramatic move really. Then he drew his sword and laid it at Mack's feet. "I am yours."

While that was happening, Paddy made another try at stabbing Valin, and Stefan had to deflect the blade with a stick he had time to fetch.

"I know the way," Valin said. "We shall all return to our present day. The breach has been healed! The wrong has been undone! My patrimony is assured! My family's shame is negated! I am free! Free as never before!"

Valin went on with more of that, but Mack kind of stopped listening. He was going to need a bit more time to get over the fact that Valin had very nearly killed him. But he needed Valin, and sometimes, when necessity demands it, you have to move past your petty grudges.

"Swell," Mack said. As they headed off to the lake where they had first emerged in this time and place, Mack pulled Xiao aside. "What was it that Sean Patrick was about to say to Boguslawa?"

"That he has been taking classes from a man who hopes to pass his business on to Sean Patrick. A man who hopes Sean Patrick will be like the son he never had and carry the honored family name forward."

"Are you about to tell me . . . ?"

Xiao nodded. "Yes. Sean Patrick has been apprentice to a clown."

"Um . . ."

"He says if he studies hard and gets good enough, he will inherit the title of . . . Izmir the Clown."

"Whatever you do—" Mack warned.

"Not a word to Valin," Xiao swore. "Not a word."

Paddy "Nine Iron" Trout was at a loss. He didn't want to live in the year 1634. There were medications and ointments in the twenty-first century that he would have a hard time finding here. On the other hand, he also didn't want to face the wrath of the Pale Queen when she learned he had let Valin join the Magnificent Twelve.

He thought it over quickly, but by the time he reached a conclusion the next morning, he was alone.

Fifteen

The Magnificent Eight . . . Wait, let's check that: Mack, Jarrah, Xiao, Dietmar, Sylvie, Rodrigo, Charlie, and Valin. Yes, eight.

The Magnificent Eight plus Stefan were face-to-face with the reality that time was just about up. And they were still eight and not twelve. If you know anything about math, you'll agree that meant they were short by four.

And bad things were brewing. The news report on the hotel TV was alarming enough even if you didn't suspect what was behind it: a volcano was forming in the ocean off San Francisco.

You know the last time a volcano formed off the coast of San Francisco? Probably the Jurassic period. There would have been dinosaurs saying, "Hey, what's that?"

There were no dinosaurs around now, just the BBC on the television at the hotel where most of the Magnifica had spent their time trying to figure out what had happened to Mack, Xiao, and Stefan.

"The dome is growing at an incredible rate, according to volcanologists. The ash plume is already drifting over the city, and California may experience major earthquakes and tidal waves. But first, we have the results of the cricket match between Kenya and Sri Lanka."

"Are you guys thinking what I'm thinking?" Mack asked.

"That I never did get those lentils?" Stefan said. He nodded angrily. "Yeah. That's what I'm thinking."

"Could this volcano be a manifestation of the Pale Queen?" Xiao suggested.

"It's awfully coincidental," Charlie said.

Sylvie said, "Can it not be said that all of life is a coincidence?" Then she thought it over and answered her own question. "No. I think this is the Pale Queen."

"Then we know where we have to go. But we don't have time to search the world for the remaining four."

"We fight the Pale Queen with just the eight of us?" Dietmar asked skeptically. "I understood that even with all twelve we would be unlikely to win. With eight we are surely doomed."

"That's right, Captain Optimist," Jarrah said.

"Here's my idea," Mack said. "We know we're being followed on YouTube by all kinds of people. For example, the Lepercon battle has been viewed more than 'Nyan Cat' and a quarter as much as 'Gangnam Style.' And the Eiffel Tower thing is really blowing up, too."

"It was trending on Twitter for days," Rodrigo said. "Up until the Taylor Swift slap fight with Justin Bieber."

"Then it's time we put all that fame to use," Mack said. "We need to send out a call for the remaining four to get to San Francisco!"

"But a bunch of nerds and weirdos will show up," Charlie argued.

"He's right," Dietmar said. "How do we make sure only the right people, the four who possess the *enlightened puissance*, show up?"

"Simple," Valin said, speaking up for the first time. He was not the least abashed about having practically tortured and nearly killed Mack. He seemed to think all was right with the world now. "If I understand Mack, he's suggesting we make a YouTube appeal. Well then, we give them a Vargran spell that will transport them to San Francisco. It will only work for those who have the true *enlightened puissance*."

Everyone nodded. Mack was even less happy about Valin coming up with a smart solution than he was when Dietmar did it. Dietmar was annoying, but he had never tried to get ants to bite Mack to death.

"Yes," Mack said. "We put out a video. Like I said." Then added, "It was my idea."

"It will need to attract attention," Rodrigo argued. "It will have to be something people want to watch."

"Huh," Stefan said, and snapped his fingers. What he meant was, "We get Taylor Swift to slap Mack!"

"Um . . . maybe not that," Mack said. "We need to figure out the Vargran we need to transport ourselves to San Francisco. And then? We just keep the video rolling."

"Who has the longest arms?" Jarrah asked.

That turned out to be Stefan. So Stefan held the phone out at arm's length, and the nine of them crammed close together to all get into the picture. And once the video was rolling, Mack looked at the camera and began to speak.

"We are the Magnifica. Well, plus Stefan here. You may remember us from such videos as 'Flying Eiffel Tower' and 'Loch Ness Duck' and, especially, 'The Cheese-filled Lepercons of Beijing.' Well, now we have a great opportunity for you. There are four more of us out there, somewhere. Four twelve-year-olds with the *enlightened puissance*. We need you to join us in a final battle with the terrifying forces of evil that will almost certainly kill us all. So if that sounds like a good time . . ."

This was not coming out quite the way he had planned.

"But we also have some fun together," he added lamely. "It's not all danger and death. Anyway, look, unless you want to spend the rest of your life being dominated by the Pale Queen and her evil—attractive, sure, but evil—daughter, Risky, you have to come and help us."

At this point Xiao took pity on Mack's rambling and laid it out. "We will give you words of the Vargran tongue. If you speak them, and if you have the *enlightened puissance*, they will be a magical spell that will transport you instantly to San Francisco."

"Just like we're about to do," Dietmar said. "If you don't believe us, just watch."

At that point Stefan shifted the camera because his arm was getting tired. The Magnifica formed up again, and Rodrigo did a countdown. *"Tres . . . dos . . . uno!"*

Eight voices chanted the words as one: *"Fla-ma ik ag San Francisco!"*

And just like that—as the soon-to-be-famous video showed—they were in San Francisco. In fact, they were in Golden Gate Park, where a thrown Frisbee hit Mack in the back of his head.

"We could have spared ourselves a lot of airline miles if we'd thought of that earlier," Jarrah pointed out.

"Upload that video," Mack instructed Stefan. "Then let's find some food."

Lingering in the restaurant after a massive lunch of sourdough pizza, sourdough soup, sourdough cioppino, and sourdough bread pudding—they'd been through a lot, so they were entitled—they checked the YouTube video. It already had tens of thousands of hits. And many comments, most of which were along the lines of, "This is a fake!" And also, "I tried the stupid spell and it didn't work!" And of course, "Aaaarrggh GUHGUHGUH Pooooooo!"

But then, the YouTube comments section is not a place where geniuses hang out.

Xiao said, "Where might these new Magnifica arrive? It's a big city, after all."

"Right where we popped in?" Jarrah suggested.

"Maybe," Dietmar said doubtfully.

Valin, with a mysterious look, said, "They will arrive where most needed."

Sylvie rolled her eyes. Valin might be her half brother, but he had tried to kill Mack, and she did not like that at all. "That is wishful thinking. A superficial analysis at best."

"Ha. I am descended from Taras Bulba. Don't tell me I'm superficial!"

146

Xiao and Mack exchanged a guilty look.

Then Mack glanced up from the table to notice that three separate smartphones were taping them. "It seems like we're being watched everywhere now."

"Makes it easy for other Magnifica to find us," Charlie said. "Of course it makes it easy for the bad guys, too."

There was a television above the bar and Dietmar said, "Shush!" in that pushy way he had. And then, equally pushy, he said loudly, "Can you turn it up, Mr. Tavern Keeper?"

The man at the bar stared hard at Dietmar but turned up the TV anyway. What had drawn Dietmar's gaze was a newscast. The video was amazing: in just the space of a few hours the boiling water and plume of ash had become a definite volcanic cone sticking up out of the ocean.

And something else: a ridge of rock was rising from the sea as well, a long spur of wave-washed stone running straight as an arrow and pointing directly at San Francisco.

Just then the ground shook beneath their feet. Dishes rattled, a bottle of soda toppled over, a waiter lost his balance and dropped his tray, and food went flying.

"That felt like a five, maybe five point one," the bartender said.

The waiter, already busy picking up the dropped dishes, said nonchalantly, "Nah, four point eight, tops. I can't believe I dropped a tray for a lousy four point eight."

The TV, which had wobbled a bit during the brief earthquake, had switched to an aerial shot that clearly showed the stony ridge as a long line of gray rocks, some already above water, much just a shadow beneath the water, and the rest only implied.

"She's building a path, a bridge," Mack said. "She's coming right this way. The Pale Queen will come out of that volcano and head straight down that rocky bridge!"

Xiao frowned. "What was it Grimluk told you? About a bridge?"

"Different bridge," Mack said. "He was talking about the Golden Gate. That's why we came to San Francisco."

"Yes, but didn't he tell you that's where we would find the remaining Magnifica?"

"Do you think he meant specifically the bridge? The bridge itself?" Mack looked around to see if anyone had any better ideas. None did.

"It will take a while for the YouTube to reach—" Valin began, but at that moment the ground beneath their feet seemed to leap to life.

The entire table jumped. Sylvie fell off her chair. Jarrah jumped to her feet but her knees buckled. Bottles and glasses fell all around them. The plate glass window cracked.

The TV went dark; the lights wavered, brightened eerily, then went out altogether.

People screamed. One of those people was Mack, who now found himself in a tangle on the floor with Sylvie and Xiao. And that floor was still very active, bucking like a rodeo horse, bruising Mack's knees and the palms of his hands. He wanted to use his hands to cover his ears because the shaking, rumbling, and groaning of the earth sounded like the end of the world.

The quake went on forever. Or maybe three minutes. But it feels like forever when you're in the middle of an earthquake.

The floor tile between Mack's hands cracked and

split, revealing the wood beneath.

The quake stopped suddenly.

Mack was breathing hard. All of them were breathing hard. Dietmar looked as pale as a ghost. He was always pale, but now even his lips were the color of vanilla ice cream.

Mack climbed shakily to his feet to see Jarrah high-fiving Stefan. "Now that was a quake!" she said excitedly. "I hope no one's hurt."

"Yeah. As long as no one's, like, dead, it was way cool," Stefan agreed.

Because honestly, those two? They were just not hooked up right.

Even Valin looked upset. And he was still at least 50 percent evil, so you'd have thought he wouldn't be upset. But he was. He had his sword drawn and was jumping around all twitchy like he was expecting an attack.

"Now, that'd be a good six point four," the bartender said, beginning to reshelve some bottles.

"Five bucks says it's not that high," the waiter demurred. "Okay, six point three is the over-under. Six point four or over, and you win."

"Deal," the bartender said.

San Francisco folks can be strange.

"Are you kidding?" Mack cried shrilly. "That was a huge earthquake!"

The waiter looked at him pityingly. "Young dude, that was a big one, but that was not the Big One by a long shot. Every full point on the Richter scale is an order of magnitude bigger. So, like, a five is not just a little bigger than a four. A five is ten times bigger than a four. Now, if the Big One ever hits, that'll be more like an eight point five. Maybe even an eight point seven. Get to nine and the whole city slides into the bay."

The bartender nodded. "Yeah, kid, if you're cleaning up broken glass, it's not the Big One. When the Big One comes, we'll be cleaning up bodies."

Despite this cheerful talk, the eight Magnifica plus Stefan decided to pay their bill and get out of there. Out on the street Mack saw very little evidence of the quake. Maybe a new crack in the street. But suddenly the horror of their situation was coming home to him in a very real way. He looked around at the buildings, at the street, at the cars, and especially at the people— none of whom were panicking but all of whom looked shaken up—and realized that what was coming was infinitely worse. Many orders of magnitude worse.

A thousand times worse.

And it was his job to stop it from happening.

"We can't just wait here eating sourdough bread and crabmeat," Mack said. He crossed his arms over his chest and planted his feet wide. People seeing this probably assumed this was his "strong leader" look. In fact his feet were planted wide apart in case the ground started moving again. And his arms were crossed because they were trembling so badly it was the only way to avoid looking like some twitchy crazy person.

He was scared. The locals might be able to shrug off an earthquake, but that was because they thought it was all over.

It was far from over.

It hadn't even begun. And when it did truly get going, when the hordes of the Pale Queen reached this city, there would be screams and terror, blood and pain and death.

"We can't just wait for her to come. We're going after her," Mack announced.

"But we are still just eight," Charlie pointed out.

"Eight is better than none," Mack said. It made no sense, really, but he said it with a very firm jaw and a very resolute voice, so it would go down in history as one of those things great heroes say that are kind of dumb but sound cool anyway.

"We are going to fight her every step of the way," Mack said. "We're going to need a boat."

Which is how the Magnificent Eight ended up on a sailboat named *The Cornucopia* captained by a woman named Grace—who accepted a cool fifty grand charged to the million-dollar credit card—and headed that lumpy craft into the bay, and beneath the majestic Golden Gate Bridge, and straight out into the Pacific Ocean.

Sixteen

The Cornucopia was a pretty big sailboat, with vast triangular sails pulling at a mast that seemed to go up a long way. Grace was pretty big herself, a seafaring sort of woman with salt-bleached blond hair and a face that had seen a few storms.

She had no crew at the moment, so Stefan had been drafted. On her orders he raced back and forth, cranking this and hauling that and tying off something else, all resulting in the boat moving pretty fast toward the Golden Gate Bridge.

The Golden Gate Bridge is like the Eiffel Tower in that both are very well-known, no surprises, but both are still very cool. It's a suspension bridge, which means that the road part basically hangs from wires. The wires hang from massive cables, which are in turn sort of draped over two very tall towers.

Some people think those wires and that cable are just there for show. They aren't. If you started cutting those wires, or worse yet, one of the two cables, the road and the cars on it would go plunging many feet down into the swift current of the Golden Gate.

Mack thought uneasily about this as the boat passed beneath the bridge. It was both big and fragile, somehow. You could imagine some giant with a giant pair of scissors cutting through those wires.

Mack was unfortunately very good at imagining terrible things. It was probably related to his many phobias. Imagination is great, but it can also torture you.

The deck of the boat was already tilted but it heeled over much farther once they passed beyond the shelter of the bay. It was pitched now almost like a roof.

"One hand for yourself and one for the boat!"

Grace yelled as Charlie and Sylvie slid like out-of-control skateboarders. Then, "Stefan! Take up the slack in that line."

It was a beautiful thing, Mack realized: a beautiful boat in a beautiful place under a beautiful blue sky dotted with scudding white clouds.

In fact it might be the most beautiful place he'd ever been. This fact just filled him with longing for home. He missed his mom and dad even if they didn't realize he was gone. He missed his boring teachers, and even more the good teachers. He missed lying around playing games online. He missed being dragged to Target to buy underwear or whatever.

None of that was ever going to happen to him again, he thought. His life was permanently messed up. Even if he somehow survived, he would always be Mack of the Magnifica.

Would he end up like Grimluk? Would he live on and on somehow? End up in some cave somewhere talking via bright chrome toilet objects to some kid in the distant future?

Sylvie came and stood beside him as he stared pensively toward the rising volcano with its plume of ash.

"What are you thinking?" Sylvie asked him.

"Me?" His first instinct was to deny that he was thinking at all. But that wouldn't do. "I'm thinking that one way or the other we're finally getting to the end."

Sylvie nodded thoughtfully. "Life? Or death? Victory or failure?"

"Yeah, all that."

"It is a beautiful day to die," she said.

Mack sighed. "Kind of early though. I mean, in terms of life. Twelve years old isn't supposed to be the end."

"Death is welcome only to those in unendurable pain," Sylvie said.

Which sounded very profound to Mack, but not very comforting. "If I die, it means I'll never go to college. Or have a job. Or eat caviar. Not that caviar sounds all that great, but everyone should taste it before they die, right?"

Sylvie moved beside him and put her arm around his waist, which left him no real choice but to do the same to her. She felt very small. It suddenly occurred to him that she would also very likely die, and that somehow seemed outrageous to him. It made him mad.

This wasn't just about Mack MacAvoy, it was about these friends of his. And his whole family back home in Sedona. All his old friends.

Also people he kind of knew but didn't really know, like people on TV shows and in movies and pop stars and all.

And then there were the billions of people he didn't know, and didn't even "kind of" know—all those people all around the world who were just minding their own business, eating lentils and driving their kids to school and doing their jobs.

"Is there not one special thing you would miss, Mack?" Sylvie asked him.

Her head was turned toward him now, and frankly she was unusually close. Closer than she had ever been before. Closer than any girl—or boy for that matter— had ever been before.

"Um . . . ," Mack said, and suddenly found he had a hard time swallowing properly.

"Is there not one thing you will miss above all others?" Sylvie asked, and her voice was breathy and kind of unsteady and her eyes were very big and he could actually feel the vibration of her heart beating.

He thought frantically. What did she mean? Was she talking about food? Was she talking about the next *Avengers* sequel that he might never see?

He didn't have the answer, but he had a feeling that maybe he did, or maybe he would if his brain was working right, which it obviously wasn't, so instead of saying, "Toaster Strudel?" which was one thing he would really, really miss, he said:

"Errr, uhhh . . ."

Sylvie's eyes closed. And she touched her lips to his.

They were extremely, extremely, extremely soft lips. Extremely.

And then she released him and walked away, swaggering just a bit.

Five minutes later Mack remembered to breathe.

And then he muttered, "Well, I didn't know I was going to miss that most. But now I do."

"Land ho!" Grace yelled.

It was not the volcano; they weren't quite there yet, although the sky was darkening with ash. It was the rising ridge of gray-and-tan stone. It was a low wall beside the boat now, getting taller as the boat blew on toward the volcano.

"Here!" Mack yelled. "This will do."

Grace ordered Stefan to drop the sails, and speed fell away. As they slowed, the choppiness of the waves became more pronounced. Mack could feel the beginnings of seasickness.

"Here, guys," he said to the others. "Any nearer to the volcano and we'd have to climb up the side of a cliff."

"We can use Vargran to—" Jarrah said.

But Mack shook his head. "Vargran is our only weapon. We only use the *enlightened puissance* when we absolutely need to. We'll jump."

Well, that proved easier in theory than it was in reality. Try jumping from a heaving boat onto a wave-washed boulder. Only Jarrah and Stefan made it without a bruise or a dunking.

Mack very nearly drowned but was rescued by Stefan and propped up on what was clearly a living, growing stone road that ran from the volcano toward the city. It would be mere hours before the road stretched all the way.

Mack knew what was coming then. Or at least some of what was coming then.

There were news helicopters in the air thwack-thwacking around shooting video of the volcano but also now of the gaggle of nine kids.

There were other aircraft as well. Two Air National Guard jets roared by overhead. A military drone circled slowly. And of course Mack could guess that up in orbit satellites aimed their cameras down at the impossible sight.

"What's the plan, boss?" It was Jarrah. She had to shout to be heard over the crashing waves, the low groan of growing rock, and the eggbeater helicopters.

"The plan?" Mack wondered aloud. He considered it, painfully aware that all eyes were on him. "Gandalf on the bridge in Khazad-dûm."

Everyone but Dietmar stared blankly. The German boy actually smiled. He had gotten the reference.

"The Pale Queen," Mack said, "shall not pass."

Seventeen

"How do we do this?" Xiao asked. "What is our strategy?"

Mack looked around at his little group: Jarrah and Stefan both grinning in anticipation of a good fight; Xiao and Sylvie both thoughtful and concerned; Dietmar looking tougher than Dietmar tended to look. Rodrigo was ostentatiously checking his fingernails, but his hands were trembling just a little. Charlie was pale and gulping a lot, and he kept kind of jerking his head like he was talking to himself and trying to encourage himself.

Valin stood a little apart, perhaps sensing that the group still resented him over his previous efforts to murder Mack. But Mack had no doubt that Valin would stand and fight. He had no doubt about any of them, really.

"I'm proud of you guys," Mack said. He hadn't meant to say it; it just came out.

For once Sylvie did not feel the need to wax philosophical and just said, "We are proud to be with you."

"Okay, then," Mack said. "We all know the problem: the *enlightened puissance* gets depleted when you use it. So we need to take turns with Vargran. We need to try and guess when it will take combined powers and when we can do things alone. And—"

At that moment he was interrupted by a vibration on the air and in the rock beneath his feet. It was not an earthquake. It was the sound of stamping feet.

Mack shaded his eyes and peered toward the volcano. Something was moving. A something made up of many smaller somethings.

An army was on the march. And it marched pretty fast.

A news helicopter swooped down to get a closer look. There was a flash of light from the moving mass, and the helicopter erupted in a ball of fire.

"No!" Sylvie cried.

From the Coast Guard cutter that had been stationed near the volcano came an amplified voice, an authoritative female voice saying, "This is the US Coast Guard. You will stop your advance and stand down immediately."

Needless to say, the vibration of booted feet never faltered. There was no hesitation. In fact, a massive spear, bigger than any human could possibly hope to carry, let alone throw, arced through the air, flew the hundred yards to the cutter, and stabbed right through the ship's bridge.

The cutter had guns. A .50 caliber machine gun and a three-inch cannon. Both erupted.

BOOOM!

BapBapBapBapBapBap!

Cannon shells flew and exploded against an invisible barrier. The bullets bounced off and dappled the water.

The ship was coming closer to where Mack and

the others stood, near enough now that they could see individual faces on the deck. Near enough that they could see medical personnel working frantically on the bridge, where the tree-trunk spear was stuck.

The firing never stopped, but suddenly, as if in response, two massive Gudridan, impossibly strong, their fur pink with fury, leaped across the hundred yards of sea and landed with a resounding thump on the ship, which suddenly seemed much smaller than it had.

One of them yanked the massive spear free, tossed it into the air, and caught it in his paw in such a way that he could stab it downward.

The other Gudridan grabbed the guardsmen at the cannon and simply threw them into the sea. He did the same with the machine gunner, who had bravely turned his weapon on the Gudridan.

The firing stopped and the two Gudridan proceeded to rip the ship apart with brute strength. A single lifeboat was launched. Guardsmen leaped into the water, but others the Gudridan caught and . . . well, there's no need to go into that, but it caused Charlie and Xiao both to look away from the horror.

The leading elements of the monstrous attack were now clearly visible. Mack saw Tong Elves, Bowands, Skirrit, Lepercons, and more Gudridan. And other creatures whose names he had never learned, terrible beasts with slavering red mouths and talons as long as ram's horns and as sharp as razors.

And that was when the air force showed up.

Two F-18s roared high above, and their missiles flew with uncanny precision, hitting the stone causeway squarely in the middle of the monstrous army. The explosions were enormous. The shock wave knocked Mack back into Stefan, and sent Sylvie rolling into Rodrigo.

But the blasts had no effect. They exploded harmlessly against the invisible protective barrier. That barrier wrapped itself around the causeway as the monsters advanced. It was impermeable, except for a brief moment when the Gudridan leaped back ashore from the now-sinking Coast Guard boat.

Mack knew there would be more ships and more planes. But none of them would stop the Pale Queen's army. In the battle of technology versus magic, technology wasn't likely to win.

"We need weapons, not just spells," Valin said urgently.

"But what can we use against the Pale Queen's own magic?" Dietmar wondered.

"A magical weapon," Charlie said. "Right? Like something that totally doesn't exist. Something that isn't about technology."

"If it's something big, we'll probably all have to work together. That will leave us vulnerable for a while," Mack said. "Okay. Who's got an idea?"

Rodrigo said, "When we were trapped for days in the sewers of Paris, Charlie would spend his time drawing amazing things. Tanks with spikes, missiles that spray sticky bombs, jets that drop sharpened steel Frisbees. . . ."

This was not something anyone (but Rodrigo) had expected of Charlie. No one had realized he was an artist. That would have explained a lot.

"Okay, look, I've got an idea," Charlie said. "But it's crazy. And we'll need some Vargran to build it and some more to penetrate that invisible shield they've got."

He dropped to a crouch and began to quickly draw

something on a flat bit of rock.

The monster army was closer now—too close for the Magnificent Eight to be sitting around drawing the kind of stuff that got you in trouble if you did it in math class.

"Cool," Jarrah opined. "How's it work?"

"It's basically a Gatling gun, but with spears instead of bullets. Eight spear shooters arranged in a drum. And the cool thing is that the spears are on wires so they get yanked back and refired."

For a minute he was just an enthusiastic kid showing off his crazy invention. And for a minute they were all, like, "Wow, cool," with a touch of "This boy's got issues" thrown in.

"I call it . . . the Spear Gun," Charlie said. Then, when no one seemed all that impressed by the name, he shrugged and said, "I'm not good with names for things."

Mack instantly saw that there was going to be a problem with this invention, but there wasn't time for a plan B.

"Okay," Mack said. "We keep the spell simple: make this drawing real. Let's try it with Xiao, Sylvie,

Rodrigo, and Charlie since it's his idea. The rest of us are going that way." He pointed toward the rapidly advancing wall of terrible creatures. "We're going to see if we can poke a hole in the Pale Queen's barrier."

Xiao said, "Take care of yourselves. We must still attempt to be the Twelve. We can afford no losses."

Sylvie met Mack's gaze. "I can afford no loss," she said.

Mack squared his shoulders. Stefan and Jarrah stood on his right. Valin and Dietmar were on the other side.

"Let's rock this," Stefan said.

Eighteen

MEANWHILE, IN SEDONA

For a full day Risky kept the golem, er, the Destroyer isolated, far from anyone. She led him up into the hills, chased away a tentful of hippies, and set to work teaching him the details of being a Destroyer.

Most people think it's easy destroying things. But . . . well, okay, actually it is easy to destroy things. Any idiot can destroy something. But the golem, er,

Destroyer wasn't just any idiot.

And Risky found herself sadly unable to teach him much because 1) the Destroyer did not pay attention, and 2) Risky didn't know much about destroying things in the modern world. She had picked up most of her destruction skills thousands of years earlier while attempting to find Gil Gamesh and bring him back to suffer her mother's wrath. So her advice on the art of destruction tended to be things like 1) set the thatched roofs afire, and 2) release the donkeys, and 3) cause the rivers to run red with blood. Which was all great if you had thatched roofs, donkeys, and a river, but Sedona had none of the above.

Risky wasn't quite ready at first to make her own move in Sedona. She wanted the entire country's attention turned on her mother's more colorful exploits in San Francisco. No one was going to even give Sedona a second look while there were monsters belching forth from a volcano just off the Golden Gate.

Well, except for the people of Sedona. They would probably object when Risky executed her nefarious plan, but this was Sedona—not some tough city like Chicago or Fort Worth or Bakersfield, where people could be expected to be hostile. Sedona was a small, peaceable place whose major industries were bead stringing, cactus cultivation, and the manufacture of dream catchers.

Still, despite her nickname, Risky didn't want to take any risks. For all she knew, the Magnificent Twelve might have fully assembled.

Strangely enough, now that she had finalized her own plans, she kind of hoped the Magnificent Twelve *had* assembled. For a long, long time now Risky had been a (basically) supportive daughter. But somehow, since her first encounter with Mack, she'd begun to wonder.

The thing was, the more she'd run into Mack, the more he had come to remind her of Gil. Not in terms of looks or muscle tone or ability to really rock the whole armor look, but in other ways. They both had a sense of humor. They both had spunk. They both foolishly believed they could defy her.

And when Risky thought of Gil, she remembered that it was her mother who had broken them up. Sort of. If her mother hadn't demanded that ridiculous temple . . . and then taken offense at the massive statue of Pikachu and demanded Gil be dismembered, Risky and he might have eventually been reconciled.

They might have had a loving and mature relationship. Until Gil aged, because, let's face it, he was mortal, and sooner or later his looks would go and then she'd eat him.

Nevertheless, Risky and Gil could have had something lovely together. Something Risky had never had. Something she'd never even thought about since then. Until she'd met Mack.

All Risky had really wanted to do with Gil was be with him by the rivers of Babylon and remember the good times they'd had together in Zion. She wept a little when she thought of it.

The thing was, obviously the world and all its people should be ruled by a domineering, iron-fisted, twisted, evil, heartless overlord. No sensible person would argue with that. But Risky didn't see why it should be the Pale Queen: Mother of Monsters, when it could just as easily be her, Risky: Fabulous Redhead.

Although she would have to make people call her Ereskigal when they worshipped her, not Risky. Queen Ereskigal.

Step One would be to await the outcome of the battle between her mother and the Magnificent Twelve. Risky was supposed to be there for that and to help her mother out, but she could always say she forgot. If her mother prevailed, well, Risky might be able to rush in and finish off a weakened Pale Queen.

And if Mack prevailed? He would come back here, to his home, to Sedona. And then Risky would convince him to join her, thus eliminating the threat of the Magnificent Twelve, and rule the world on her own.

Sweet.

But she would need to lay the trap first so Mack didn't have advance warning. For that, she needed her Destroyer.

"Okay, Destroyer," Risky said, prodding him with her toe. (He was lying on the ground.) "Time to get back to town. My mother's assault on All That Is Good and Decent is well under way. Time for me to get busy."

"Urgh," the golem Destroyer said. He was not talkative.

"The first thing we have to do is empty the town. We need everyone to flee!"

The Destroyer considered this for a moment. "Flee where?"

"Out into the desert," Risky said cruelly. "I don't want Mack finding any support or any help at all. None!"

"Okay," the Destroyer said.

But Risky didn't like that. It sounded way too casual for a Destroyer. "You should say something like, 'I obey!' Or maybe, 'All will worship you, mighty princess.'"

"Urgh."

She was asking the Destroyer to make a choice, and that wasn't going to work.

"You have no initiative, do you know that?" Risky snarked. "Okay, do this. Whenever I give you an order, you say, 'I obey the will of Ereskigal!'"

"But all your friends call you Risky," the Destroyer said.

Risky smiled an evil smile and her green eyes glowed vindictively. "I have no friends."

Ah, but once upon a time, long, long ago, she had.

LONG, LONG AGO
WHEN RISKY HAD A FRIEND

The opening of the temple went better than Risky had expected. The various animal sacrifices were successful—as you could see from the large copper bowl of hearts and the barrels of blood. The blood gutters worked just as well as Gil had promised.

The Pale Queen complained that the temple was drafty. But Risky was used to her mother belittling everything she did. If Risky destroyed a village, the Pale Queen would point out the one pigsty Risky missed. She had always been critical of Risky. Nothing was ever good enough.

But by the standards of the Pale Queen, her reaction to her new temple was pretty good.

Until the unveiling of the statue.

Oy. That didn't go well.

So in a rage the Pale Queen devoured the sculptors and demanded she be given Gil to chew on as well.

But where was Gil? Gil had totally disappeared, it seemed. And now, the worm of doubt entered Risky's thoughts. One of two things had happened. Either the Pale Queen had already eaten Gil, possibly without even knowing who he was. Or . . .

Or Gil had run off with another girl!

"Mom?" Risky demanded, hands on hips and staring up at her mother's bloodstained mouth. (She was snacking on the big bowl of unicorn hearts, like someone with a bowl of cashews.) "Did you kill my boyfriend?"

"Your what?"

"My boyfriend," Risky said defiantly. "Gil. The architect who designed this temple. I love him, Mom, and if you ate him I am going to be really mad."

"You're too young to be dating!" the Pale Queen roared, which sent red spittle flying everywhere.

"I'm a thousand years old, Mother!"

"Nonsense. If you're a thousand years old, then I'm . . ." The Pale Queen glanced at her not-exactly-lifelike statue as if seeking reassurance that she was still young and beautiful. (If by *young* you meant two thousand years old and if by *beautiful* you meant a terrifying, tyrannosaurus-jawed, claw-handed, snake-eyed monster drenched in nine different kinds of blood.)

"Just tell me if you ate Gil Gamesh!" Risky cried.

"No. I don't think so. Are there any mirrors in this place?"

Risky ran from the temple determined to find Gil, to tell him of her love, and then most likely torture him for running out on her. But though she searched and searched, from Babylon to Erech to far-off Kom Ombo, and though she transformed herself into a huge bird of prey with incredible eyesight and flew over Mesopotamia, Egypt, Assyria, Cappadocia, Hyrcania, and other places that were totally real but so exotic that they would be unrecognized by spell-check far in the future, she could not find him.

Risky as a lonely hawk became a familiar sight over the fields of Lydia, and her harsh birdlike cry, "Gil . . . squaaaaawk . . . Gil!" haunted the dreams of children in far-away Thracia.

Slowly, slowly, her heart hardened. Sadness and loss and the frustration that came from not being able to hear Gil's loving words and/or cries of pain would leave their mark on Risky.

It was as if her heart had been frozen stiff. And nothing would begin to thaw that cold, cold heart until she first met Mack.

Who she was now totally probably going to kill.

Unless, of course, he was willing to help her rule the world through terror.

Nineteen

Here is the scene. The volcano's cone now rose seven hundred feet above the agitated waves. A pillar of smoke rose all the way to the stratosphere.

Lava belched from several different holes in the volcano and rolled red-hot and sluggish down to the water, where it sent up clouds of searing steam. The lava cooled, darkened, and formed new additions to the volcano.

On the eastern face of the volcano a jagged hole made it seem as if the volcano had a mouth. It was a dark hole from which marched the Pale Queen's terrible army.

The stone causeway continued to rise from the sea and now came near to reaching to the Golden Gate Bridge itself. It grew almost as if it was something living, summoned from the bottom of the ocean. The causeway was perhaps four miles long in all, making it quite visible from land. And, indeed, TV cameras and phone cameras and every kind of camera in between showed pictures that left the whole country, the whole world, staring in helpless horror.

Marines and soldiers were being rushed to San Francisco by truck and plane and helicopter, but the nearest hardcore combat soldiers were about 450 miles away. And really all that San Francisco had at the moment were the San Francisco Police Department, the California Highway Patrol, and a handful of National Guardsmen.

Coming down that causeway there were two miles' worth of bad creatures. The Pale Queen had concentrated her shock troops for this attack. Although there were reports coming in of smaller attacks in Europe, Asia, Africa, and South America.

Roughly at the midpoint of the causeway stood the Magnificent Eight. The Pale Queen's army would have to get past them to reach the city and the world beyond. But if you were to look at it from the air, as the various TV cameras in helicopters were doing, it wouldn't look like much of a contest. A massive, marching monster army versus nine kids.

Xiao, Sylvie, Rodrigo, and Charlie were summoning the killing weapon that Charlie had imagined. It was assembling itself out of thin air, piece by piece. Clearly it would be an incredible thing when fully built. It stood on a tripod that looked as if it was made of elephant tusks twisted together. It resembled some massive machine gun, but a very old-school version with long, glittering barrels arranged in a cylinder. There was no knowing just what the building materials were—perhaps they weren't real metals or minerals at all. They were pure imagination, the result of a bored English schoolkid scribbling away when he should have been studying English history.[38]

---

38 There's a whole lot of English history. Unless you really like history, you should go to school in a country with a shorter history, like the United States or Australia. Or a country where nothing ever happens, like Canada or Switzerland.

Something about Charlie's machine almost seemed to suggest it might be alive, and some elements of it looked more like knuckles or ligaments than steel.

Mack, Jarrah, Dietmar, Valin, and Stefan were marching the totally wrong way, which is to say toward the onrushing fist of terrifying creatures. No more than three hundred feet separated Mack from certain destruction. Maybe less, because one of the Gudridan in the lead launched a three-pointed spear through the air.

It flew straight and true toward Mack. But Mack was quick. He jumped to his left, expecting the spear to stick in the rock where he'd just been.

Instead, a muscular hand, quick as a snake, shot out and grabbed the shaft of the spear. The forward momentum of the heavy weapon twisted Stefan around but did not knock him down.

He switched the spear to his right hand, took three running steps, and hurled it right back at the surprised Gudridan.

But the spear clattered off the invisible force field, and the Gudridan smiled. (Which is not something you want to see.)

"No fair," Stefan said, honestly outraged. "They can throw at us and we can't throw back?"

"That's what we're here to fix," Mack said, trying to sound all tough and indifferent to fear.

"*Krik-ma* is 'break,'" Jarrah said.

"*Poindrafol* is 'shield,'" Dietmar said.

"Is that a shield?" Mack asked. "We've seen what happens when you're not specific enough." He was referring to the fact that he'd needed to specify that Valin was using a scimitar, not just any old sword.

Valin smiled tightly. "You really don't know much, do you, my ancient enemy—I mean, well, Mack. Use the prefix *simu*. It means 'like.' *Simu-poindrafol* should mean 'thing like a shield.'"

"Grab hands, now or never!" Jarrah cried, because at that moment the advancing army decided they were tired of walking and broke into a run.

Mack held Jarrah's hand and she Dietmar's and he Valin's, while Stefan scowled fearlessly at doom.

"*Krik-ma simu-poindrafol!*"

The next three things happened very fast and almost all together.

1) A sheen of bright blue light seemed to outline and define the barrier, which was revealed as a sort of

long tube that ran the length of the Pale Queen's army.

The light did not disappear. But at the front, at the part between Mack and the mad beasts, an emptiness appeared, a hole.

2) The first row of monsters surged like a crashing wave. They came on with a weird melding of awful war cries, ranging from the Skirrit's metallic locust sound to the Tong Elves' deep-throated bellowing of their tong names. The Bowands, those thin bow-handed creatures, screeched like boiled cats and fired their deadly darts. The Gudridan made a tigerish huffing sound.

3) Charlie yelled, "Fire!" A shaft as long as a basketball player and as thick as a beach umbrella's pole shot over Mack's head. It went straight through a leaping Gudridan, then a Tong Elf, then two more Tong Elves and a Skirrit.

The spear trailed a wire that snapped tight, stopping the weapon's flight. Prongs snapped out of the side of the spearpoint, and the whole thing went flying back, reeled in faster than a yo-yo.

A Skirrit, three Tong Elves, and a Gudridan were impaled like some hideous shish kebab, yanked wildly back toward Charlie's machine.

Mack had foreseen a problem with this: Charlie's

speargun would soon be buried in dead monsters. But the instant the monsters cleared the protection of the invisible barrier, they exploded into vapor.

The spear was sucked back into its barrel bearing no traces of the monsters that had just been killed.

"Nice touch!" Mack yelled to Charlie.

"That wasn't me," Charlie yelled back, but there was no more time to discuss the matter because if you thought the Pale Queen's army would just turn and run away in terror, you'd be sadly mistaken. They had something much scarier behind them—the Pale Queen—than they had in front of them.

So after a stunned pause, the creatures charged again, loud as ever.

Mack yelled, "Back! Back behind the speargun!"

They fell back, and Rodrigo, who was operating the speargun now, cranked it up to maximum effect.

The result was slaughter.

The spears shot out one at a time, speared Bowands and bugs and giants, yanked them back, and reduced them to air pollution. The ten barrels turned in the drum, bringing a new spear into firing position every second.

In the first minute the spears flew and withdrew sixty times. The slaughter was appalling and the air was clouded with the stinking vapor left behind by the creatures' dissolution.

And yet, despite this fearsome destruction, the Pale Queen's army kept pushing forward, and soon Mack and Stefan and Dietmar were hauling the machine back, foot by foot, even as it fired frantically.

There have been many epic battles in history that involved a tiny, outnumbered band of heroes borne down upon by irresistible forces. The Spartans at Thermopylae. The English navy and the Spanish Armada. The 101st Airborne at the Battle of the Bulge. The Ewoks of Endor against the Imperial Stormtroopers.

But never in history had so few stood against so many. Eight twelve-year-olds and one fifteen-year-old ex-bully against tens of thousands.

And they were not going to win.

Not as the Magnificent Eight at least.

Twenty

MEANWHILE, BACK IN SEDONA

The Destroyer picked up an SUV—it happened
to be a Toyota RAV4, not that it matters—and
he threw that SUV—it happened to be blue—again,
not that it matters—into the front wall of a house.

The SUV crushed the front door, collapsed the
porch, shattered the window, and scared the residents
pretty well.

It was a miracle no one was hurt.

The Destroyer then kicked a fire hydrant, which snapped off clean and sent a giant plume of water spraying up into the air.

He didn't exactly know what the limits were to his power. Risky had tried to explain, but whenever he tried to pay attention, his thoughts would drift away to . . . well, he could no longer remember what to call the creature in his memory. But she was a girl, he was pretty sure of that. And she was cute edging toward pretty.

But he had no time for that now. He was the Destroyer.

The Destroyer formerly known as Mack's golem grabbed an elm tree by the trunk and heaved up on it. Sure enough it came free after some resistance, ripping out topsoil, grass, and bits of sidewalk. He opened his baleful mouth and breathed out. Flames!

But the tree didn't burn, really, not the way he'd hoped. The wood was still green and fresh so it mostly just kind of steamed and twisted. He threw the whole thing onto the roof of a pleasant stucco bungalow.

People heard loud crashes and car alarms and began to poke their heads out of their homes to see what was going on. But it wasn't nearly enough. He'd been tasked with the job of scaring everyone all the way out of town. And so far he was getting more puzzled looks than terrified ones.

So he tilted back his head and let go of a howl that sounded like, "Braaaaarrrrrgggg!" But really loud. Jet-engine loud. Rock-concert loud.

More people opened their doors and stepped outside to see what was what.

An idea popped into his head. If he were to snatch up one of those people and bite his head off, people would flee much better.

While he was thinking about this, he picked up a Mustang convertible—it happened to be black—and used it to smash another car—a brown Mercedes, not that it matters.

The noise was astonishing, and the Destroyer liked it, so he roared again, and the roaring and the car smashing brought the last few semideaf people from their homes.

Some ducked right back inside and slammed their doors.

Some began to make phone calls with shaky fingers.

Others used their phones to make videos, because that's just the way the world was nowadays.

Only one man ran, shoeless and in his boxers, to hop into the car in his driveway and go tearing down the street in terror.

This would not do. Risky would be very annoyed with him if he caused insufficient terror.

He was going to have to . . . to . . . kill.

But again, he distracted himself by breathing fire, all down the side of a moving van—Mayflower Transit—which turned to flames most gratifyingly.

Leaving flame and fire behind, the Destroyer approached a house that looked vaguely familiar. He blinked his dull eyes at the mailbox. The name on it read "MacAvoy."

Something about that seemed familiar.

He used one massive fist to crush that mailbox, but the way it was squashed left the name still readable.

The mail had spilled out. Brightly colored junk mail on slick paper. That kind of paper was tasty, but Mom had said not to eat it because then she wouldn't know all the best deals at Safeway.

She liked to wait for sales on Nutella.

The Destroyer frowned, which was not easy with a metallic face and dead, lifeless eyes. What was Nutella? What was Safeway?

What was Mom?

It was like something was in his head trying to squirm around in there and make him think about . . . about stuff. Strange stuff.

But he had no time for strange stuff. He was the Destroyer! He had a reason for existence: destruction. He had a mission: create so much destruction that everyone fled the city and Risky could lay a perfect trap for Mack.

Mack. That was another of those squirmy things in his head. What did it mean? Why was it in there?

He frowned harder still and scrunched his eyes and even pounded the side of his massive bullet head. What did that word mean?

Mack?

In frustration, the Destroyer punched a hole in the roof of the nearest car.

"Hey! Stop that!"

The Destroyer was almost relieved to have someone to vent his anger on. And there she was. A girl.

The one he'd thought of when Risky was trying to teach him about smashing idols and knocking over butter churns.

He did not know her name, but yes, she seemed familiar. He pounded the side of his head again, trying to get the faint memories either to come together and form a picture, or to go away and stop confusing him.

"Hey. Hey, it's me, Camaro," she said. She was bold, that was for sure. He stood about ten feet tall, and she was barely half that.

He tried to say that word. *Camaro.* But it came out all muddy and garbled. "Unhargo?"

"Yes, Camaro Angianelli. Duh. What do you think you're doing?"

The gole— er, Destroyer had to think about that for a minute. What was he doing? Well, he was being the Destroyer. He was scaring all the people out of town. "Chkaring peepill?"

He said it as a question. Somehow Camaro understood. (But then she always had understood him, hadn't she? Even when no one else did.)

"Scaring people? That's your answer? You're scaring people? Why?"

The Destroyer's thought process was not exactly swift. After all, he was the Destroyer, not the Jeopardy Contestant. He patted his chest with one massive fist. "I m er Geshtroer."

"You're the Destroyer?" Camaro rolled her eyes. "Why, because that dye-job redhead said so? Destroyer, please."

The Destroyer was feeling anxious. He needed to destroy. He needed to scare people. It was who he was, after all. It's what he was.

Camaro must have sensed this, for she said, "You need to destroy something? Is that it? Will you be happy if you have something to destroy? Well, there are people in all these houses. And we don't want to hurt people, do we?"

The Destroyer had to think about that for a while. Camaro lost patience waiting for him, sighed, and said, "Look, I have something you can destroy that's totally empty because it's Saturday. And it may make some people unhappy, but it will make a whole lot of kids happy."

This sounded okay to the Destroyer, who, frankly, was just weary from all the thinking. So he followed

Camaro meekly, contenting himself with kicking over the occasional trash can as they made their way several blocks to a building that, quite honestly, was pretty old and run-down and should have been replaced long ago.

And that's how Richard Gere Middle School[39] came to be utterly destroyed as the children of Sedona watched and cheered.

---

39 Go, Fighting Pupfish. No, really: go.

Twenty-one

They made the Pale Queen's forces pay a price. That they did. For a long, desperate mile, the Magnificent Eight plus Stefan fought.

Other forces joined the fight, but were helpless. The air force again bombed the column of evil, but with no effect. A second Coast Guard cutter arrived and shelled the column and also had no effect.

Two helicopters with San Francisco police SWAT teams showed up. The black-helmeted, heavily armed officers stood with the Magnificent Eight and fired steadily at the advancing horde. The bullets took a toll and, along with Charlie's speargun, slowed the advance, but not by much, and the SWAT team was running low on ammunition.

The police officer in charge, Captain Molly O'Neill, identified Mack as the leader and said, "What can we do to stop those things?"

"You can't," Mack said.

"All right then, what can you do to stop them?"

"We need more time to get our strength back," Mack said. "As you can see, we've made a hole we can shoot through, but we don't have the power to kill the whole force field."

"I've seen you online, kid: you can do plenty."

"This is different," Mack said. "She is fighting us. The Pale Queen. Her magic is in that barrier. Her determination is in all these evil creatures. We push, she pushes back."

"You telling me all is lost?" Captain O'Neill demanded.

Mack shot a glance at his friends. They had taken turns firing the speargun. In between they had grabbed up rocks and thrown them. Stefan had become very good at grabbing spears in midair and throwing them back, sometimes hitting his target. Jarrah was beside him the whole time.

"We're short four people," Mack said. "With twelve, we have a chance. With eight, all we do is lose slowly instead of quickly."

"So where are the other four?"

"Maybe in the city. Maybe not. Listen, you want to help? Put out the word through your forces, through TV, radio, everything, so that everyone in the city hears it. We're looking for some twelve-year-olds who may have just popped into the city unexpectedly. They might be a bit lost and disoriented. Find them. Get them to . . ." Mack looked back at the city, now much closer than before since they had retreated. The causeway was very close to passing beneath the Golden Gate Bridge. "To the bridge."

"The bridge?"

Mack locked eyes with Dietmar, who nodded.

"The bridge, Captain O'Neill. We'll make our stand on the Golden Gate Bridge."

The police officer nodded, squared her shoulders, and began speaking into her radio.

Xiao took Mack's arm. "I must go."

"What? What do you mean?"

"There may be something I can do," she said. "It

is time for all the forces of good to fight, whatever the risks."

She squeezed his arm and began the swift transition to her true shape. In seconds she was a dragon once more, a turquoise serpent with a fierce face, who slithered away into the sky, heading toward the city.

"Okay, what next?" Captain O'Neill demanded. Somehow a dragon had barely fazed her. It was that kind of day.

"Get hold of the Coast Guard and all the other forces, as well as your own people; tell them to focus on the front edge of the column—that's where the hole is. Take over the speargun. We need to get to the bridge."

"You're running out?"

Dietmar spoke up. "Don't be a fool! This is Mack of the Magnifica. He does not run!"

Mack was a bit taken aback by that. Even more when Valin said, "He does not run. Nor do we."

"We have one chance, Captain," Mack explained. "We get to the bridge and find the other four waiting for us. Or . . ."

"Or what?"

"Or the world is enslaved and all freedom dies."

Twenty-two

Mack led his tired, frightened forces down the causeway. It looked like retreat. It felt like retreat. The stone causeway was still growing ahead of them, rising from the sea.

An earthquake rattled them so badly it knocked them all to their knees. Mack could see the tall buildings of the city sway just ever so slightly. He saw the bridge sway even more.

Behind them the roar of gunfire and the furious cries of the Pale Queen's troops faded slowly. Mack felt terrible guilt at that. Had he just left innocent people to die?

Three heavy military helicopters swooped overhead and circled to land just behind where the SWAT team was still firing the speargun. The Coast Guard cutter was also firing steadily until a bolt of fire hit its deck gun.

The bridge loomed huge now, almost overhead. Mack saw people lining the railing, pointing, aiming cameras at the incredible battle, at the causeway, and down at his little band of Magnifica.

They had reached the just-emerging tip of the stone causeway. Any farther and they'd be walking in water. But now the causeway was doing something strange. Okay, its very existence was strange, but up until now it had just been a sort of stone roadway. Now the tip, the end of it, was piling higher and higher. The earth groaned as the stone grew.

"It's making a ramp up to the bridge!" Rodrigo said, pointing.

"It's not for us," Mack said. "We need to get up there now, ahead of that mob back there."

"Vargran?" Valin suggested, frowning.

"If we do, we're powerless again," Sylvie said. "It is the dilemma of our power: to use it is to lose it. To fail to use it is to die."

Mack usually appreciated Sylvie's philosophical musings, but in this case it was just a bit depressing.

"Look!" Jarrah cried. "It's Xiao!"

Mack squinted and looked close, thinking, I wonder if that's her? And then realized it was pretty unlikely to be some other turquoise dragon.

She came slithering beneath the bridge and landed beside them.

"Where did you get to?" Charlie asked her.

"Visiting friends and relatives," Xiao said. Had it been Jarrah, Mack would have thought it was a sarcastic answer. But Xiao wasn't really the sarcastic sort. Occasionally, but not often.

"We need to get off this causeway and onto the bridge," Mack said. "Can you help us?"

She could, but only three at a time. The last two were Mack and Stefan.

Stefan was gazing back toward the battle. The cops and marines were falling back, getting closer every second. The murdering horde was just beyond them.

Mack had the definite feeling that there might be fewer cops and marines still standing than there had been to start with.

The Coast Guard cutter was burning and veered away. A helicopter lay crumpled and sinking beneath the waves.

"You know what I said about you being under my wing?" Stefan said, not taking his eyes from the terrible conflict.

"Of course," Mack said.

Stefan looked at Mack, and to Mack's amazement there were tears in his former bully's cold blue eyes. "I don't think I can protect you from what's coming."

Mack didn't know what to say. Just then Xiao reappeared, and the two boys climbed swiftly onto her back, Stefan behind Mack.

As they rose into the air, Mack heard Stefan whisper, "But I'll make them pay."

It was a wild ride up to the bridge. The bridge is an object that is both delicate and massive. Past one end lay the brown hills of Marin County; on the other end, the green trees and hills of the Presidio park, and beyond it the city of San Francisco.

To one side of the bridge there was the bay with its sailboats and ferries and hulking great cargo ships. To the other side there was the Pacific Ocean, though something new now dominated that familiar view.

As they rose through the air on Xiao's back, Mack saw the full length of the causeway. The creatures looked small from up here. Small but not harmless. They bristled with weapons both natural and manufactured. Mack saw a creature he'd never seen before, nor imagined in his darkest nightmare: he saw the source of the firebolts that lanced out at helicopters and ships. It was a deep-red, six-legged, twisting, curling, wormlike thing with a head as smooth as a snake's but for two hornlike protrusions, one on either side. One was red and dripped liquid fire. The other was blue. As the creature moved, it casually crushed Tong Elves and Skirrit. It even dared to push aside the giant Gudridan. And unless Mack was very much mistaken, it occasionally shot out its forked tongue and sucked in a Lepercon.

It was hard to feel sorry for the Lepercons. Mack had had a run-in with them before and didn't like them one bit.

Jets now flew higher, out of the monsters' range,

and fired missiles that were no longer wasted on the impenetrable barrier but were aimed at the hole Mack and his friends had made. Two missiles arrived without more than a second's notice and flew right into that opening.

The explosion was incredible and everyone cheered, including the people who lined the rail on the bridge.

"You people need to get off this bridge!" Mack yelled, realizing that they were in great danger. In fact, he told them: "You're in great danger!"

"Hey, it's that kid from YouTube!" someone shouted, and pretty soon camera phones were swinging back and forth between Mack and the advancing army of the Pale Queen. Very few people ran away, which was certainly what Mack felt like doing.

Police had not even stopped traffic onto the bridge yet. Of course they were busy, but this, Mack knew, was a disaster in the making.

A disappointed sound went up from the onlookers as the smoke of the missiles' explosions cleared and showed the monsters still coming.

"Get off this bridge, you idiots!" Mack yelled. "Do you want to die?"

Now, finally, the people on the sidewalk—there's a sidewalk running along both sides of the bridge, wide enough for four or five people to walk abreast[40]— headed either toward the city side or the Marin side. They could clearly see that the living stone of the causeway was rising up, curling toward the bridge itself. And it was plain to see that neither missiles nor cannon nor rifles nor Charlie's speargun could stop the onslaught. The SWAT team and the few marines would be lucky to get out alive.

"Everyone, out!" Stefan yelled, and that had even more effect than Mack's warning. "Off this bridge!"

"But we have to be here," a voice said.

There were two people who looked like they might be twelve years old. One was a boy. He was black, tall, gangly, and wearing a T-shirt from the band Rancid over khaki shorts. On his feet: sandals.

It was impossible to miss the fact that he was dressed for some place warmer than San Francisco.

By the same token, it was impossible to avoid noting that the other kid was rather overdressed for the Northern California climate. She wore a hugely puffy

---

40 Most people walk a dog; some people walk abreast.

down jacket with a hood lined in fur, thick gloves, a scarf, and insulated stretch pants. She had dark goggles pushed up onto her tumbling blond hair. And, strangest of all, she was standing on a snowboard.

The boy had spoken. The girl seemed inclined to just stare.

"Who are you?" Mack demanded.

The boy answered. "I am José. Five minutes ago I was waiting for a bus in Espírito Santo."

"How did you get here?"

"You tell me," José said. "I am watching a video of you, and you gave us words to say. And here I am."

A slow smile formed on Mack's lips. "You're one of us?"

"I don't know what I am." José looked around. "Or where I am. Is this Brazil?"

"What? Why would you think . . . ? Never mind; it's San Francisco." He pointed down at the battle below. "That's the Pale Queen's army."

"Those are, like, monsters or whatever," the blond girl said. "This is not Banff." She looked around some more. "This is, like, a bridge or whatever. Monica was just showing me this stupid video and—"

Just then two missiles went arcing overhead, broke the sound barrier loudly, and hit the leading edge of the monster army.

"You're part of the Magnificent Twelve now," Mack said. "That's Jarrah, Xiao, Dietmar, Sylvie, Charlie, Rodrigo, and Valin, and I'm Mack. And that's Stefan."

"Uh, right, so I'm going to call my mom, okay? Right." The girl pulled out her phone and started to dial. "Oh great, straight to voice mail. Mom? It's Hillary and I am, like, in San Francisco and they are having some kind of war or whatever and—"

Hillary was interrupted a second time, this time when the ground began to shake. It was the most severe quake yet. The bridge swayed extravagantly. Mack fell onto his back and, looking up, saw the vertical cables like ropes being yanked and released. The main cable, the one that was as thick as a subway tunnel, vibrated and swung just a little, but that little felt like a lot down on the road itself.

The quake went on for a long and frightening while. Both of the new Magnifica were yelling and praying. The more experienced Magnifica knew they were unlikely to be killed by a quake and much more likely to eventually be clubbed, stabbed, beheaded, disemboweled, or eaten by one of the Pale Queen's minions or the queen herself.

The instant the quake settled down, Mack jumped to his feet and said, "Xiao, Jarrah, Valin: you three are strongest in Vargran; teach the new kids."

"No one is teaching me—" Hillary began, but Stefan moved in close.

"Huh," he said, meaning, "No time for nonsense." He took the phone from her hand and tossed it over the side of the bridge.

In extreme emergencies it's sometimes useful to have a bully.

"So, we are ten," Mack said to Dietmar and Sylvie.

"But not yet twelve. Will ten be enough?"

Dietmar shook his head. "I believe the *enlightened puissance* has a logarithmic rather than linear progression. Like the Richter scale."

That got him a pair of blank stares. So he explained.

"Two Magnifica are twice as powerful as one. But three may be six times as powerful as two. And four may be twelve times as powerful as one. The final two, or one, may increase our power a thousand times. Do you see?"

But seeing was about to become a problem. As so often happened in the San Francisco Bay Area, a wall of fog was advancing swiftly from the sea. It was like a great, gray fist aimed right at the Golden Gate.

It swallowed the volcano first, so that all that could be seen was a dull red glow.

It advanced up the causeway, disappearing the evil minions.

It reached the battlefront, obscuring good and evil alike and dampening and distorting the sounds of the fight.

It could totally have been just your average San Francisco fog. It could have, except for the fact that riding the fog like some kind of nightmare surfers were creatures, gigantic creatures, who seemed to have been formed of the very fog.

So, it was not exactly your average fog.

Mack pointed at this new abomination. "I think we better hope two more Magnifica show up, and fast."

Twenty-three

Power is a funny thing. You think you want it. You think it's great to be Spider-Man or the Flash or the Incredible Hulk or whatever. But power always has its drawbacks. Always.

In the case of the Magnificent Eight—wait, Ten— it was great to have the *enlightened puissance* that allowed them to use the magical Vargran language. But that meant they had to learn the Vargran language. And it meant they had to be careful in their use of *enlightened puissance* because that power had limits.

It had to be used at just the right time, and only when necessary, because if they used it on one thing, they couldn't use it on the next.

Now the Magnifica were turning to Mack, looking to him for guidance, waiting for him to give them some kind of direction. But you know what? Teachers didn't exactly teach the use of extraordinary powers in school. Mack didn't know how to make life-and-death decisions. He hadn't read a book about it or anything.

"We don't even know what to call those things," Mack said, pointing at the fog riders. "If we can't name them, we can't control them."

The fog, and the fog riders, had reached the bridge. There were still cars going by, but almost all the civilian pedestrians had gotten off the bridge. All except some handicapped boy in a wheelchair.

"Stefan! Get that kid off the bridge!" Mack yelled. "Wait! I mean, get him to safety, don't throw him off the side."

It was also best to be specific when dealing with Stefan.

Stefan ran to the wheelchair kid.

Beneath them the stone pier had now risen to the bottom of the bridge, and from the fog emerged a phalanx of Skirrit, who were the best climbers among the bad guys. They came swarming up the rough stone ramp.

At the same time the fog riders leaped onto the Marin side of the bridge and began to advance. They were built like humans but on a much larger scale. As they walked—it was more of a rolling swagger, really—they seemed to swirl in on themselves, as if they were slo-mo tornadoes made of dense steam. They had no facial features other than a suggestion of a brow, concavities where there might or might not have been eyes.

Mack shot a desperate look toward the San Francisco end of the bridge. The fog swirled up and over it, hiding the city and any illusion of safety from view.

Was that it? Did they have to flee? After all this, were they going to get their butts kicked in ten seconds, game over?

"No," Mack said. And he clenched his fists.

"No what?" Jarrah asked.

"No, we're not going to run," Mack said.

"Never thought we would," Jarrah said. She slapped Mack on the back.

"We're probably going to get killed," Mack said. "Sorry I got you all into this."

"You did not get us into this," Sylvie said. "It is fate, *n'est-ce pas?*"[41]

"We need a wind. A very big wind," Mack said, thinking out loud. "That may get rid of those fog creatures."

"It won't stop the others!" Dietmar said shrilly.

"I know!" Mack cried.

Stefan came running out of the fog pushing the wheelchair. The boy in the wheelchair had dark hair, high cheekbones, cool blue eyes, very strong shoulders, and shriveled legs. He was maybe eleven. Or thirteen.

Or.

"Also," Stefan panted as he ran up, "he says he's supposed to be here."

"You're one of us?" Mack asked.

"My name is Ilya. Yes, I am one of you. At least, I said the words and was one minute in Moscow and then, poof, here!"

---

41 French for "right?"

"Bad timing, Ilya; we're about to get slaughtered," Mack said.

"Eleven of us," Dietmar said. "Maybe . . ."

Mack nodded. "We have to try. Now or never. Who knows the word for *tornado* or *hurricane*?"

"What about the cops and the soldiers and the Coast Guard and all?" the new girl, Hillary, asked. Apparently she wasn't totally clueless.

"They're already lost," Stefan said bluntly, avoiding huh-speak. "Gotta do what we gotta do."

Mack nodded, accepting that, and secretly grateful that Stefan was the one to say it so he didn't have to.

"*Ti(ch) azor*," Xiao suggested.

"Okay, then all together, focused, all our power," Mack said. "The spell will be, *Exah-ma ti(ch) azor*. Ilya, Hillary, and José, you've never done this before. So just focus all your thoughts, picture a hurricane, and repeat all together."

"*Exah-ma ti(ch) azor!*"

Twenty-four

MEANWHILE, IN SEDONA

"You call this terrifying people?"

Risky had arrived without her usual fanfare, just walked up to the school. Or what was left of the school. Because Richard Gere Middle School[42] was a very large heap of rubble.

Risky approved of the destruction. But she did not approve of the way people were standing around

---

42 Ouch, Fighting Pupfish!

watching. She was quite frankly disturbed by the way someone had set up a hibachi and was cooking popcorn in a large kettle and selling it for a dollar fifty for a one-gallon Ziploc bagful.

"This is not terror," Risky complained. "This is just destruction."

The gole— er, Destroyer looked as sheepish as it is possible to look when you're ten feet tall and incapable of facial expressions.

Risky stood with hands on hips and glared at him. "How many people have you killed or dismembered?"

"Urrrr," the Destroyer mumbled.

"Do not stand there and tell me you haven't killed or dismembered anyone," Risky raged. She was shaking her finger in his face.

"Hey!" Camaro Angianelli arrived back from the popcorn stand. She set her popcorn down, cracked her knuckles, rolled her shoulders, stretched her Achilles tendon, and generally got ready for a fight. "You don't yell at my boyfriend!"

"Your . . ." Risky was speechless for a moment. Then she laughed. It was one of those brittle, phony, forced laughs, not something that came from a deep well of inner mirth. Risky's innards were mirthless. This was one of those insulting laughs. "Ah-ha-ha-ha-ha-ha-ha-ha-ha." That went on too long. "Oh-ho-ho-ho-ho. You think he's your boyfriend?"

"I know what he is," Camaro said. "He's the golem who's covering for Mack while he's off saving the world."

The crowd that had gathered to watch the destruction included a number of Mack's friends—his friends were for some reason especially enthusiastic about the destruction of the school. Plus, Mack's parents had both just pulled up, gotten out of their car with the thought of stopping this destruction, and then been seduced by the smell of popcorn.

All these people—Mack's friends and parents—all said various versions of, "What are you talking about? Mack's not off saving the world."

Camaro sighed, did a facepalm,[43] and pulled out her phone.

"Do none of you people ever go on the internet?" She began loading Mack's latest YouTube video.

---

43 This involves putting the palm of your hand on your face, then sliding it slowly down while you mutter, "Give me strength." Just watch your mom or dad next time one of the pets pees in the house.

Which happened to be the one where he appealed to any hidden Magnifica out there.

She held it up and said, "See? Mack. This"—she indicated the Destroyer—"is a golem who has been covering for Mack."

"Nonsense," Mack's father said. "We would have noticed."

"Well," Mack's mother said, making a worried face, "he has been acting strangely lately. Remember how he started dripping mud when you turned on the sprinkler?"

"Also," one of the kids said, "he never used to be able to change size."

Meanwhile on the tinny little speakers of Camaro's phone, Mack was saying something in a very weird language. It sounded like, "*Fla-ma ik ag San Francisco!*"

Risky just shook her head in disbelief. "Seriously? You people are too dumb to be free. You deserve to be dominated by a ruthless overlord who will crush your pitiful spirits and turn you into terrified slaves who worship her like the goddess she is."

When everyone looked puzzled, she said, "Me. Me, duh. That's who you're going to worship. Me. But first . . ." She sighed. "I swear, if you want something done right, you have to do it yourself."

She began to change then. Her lovely, pale, barely freckled skin turned a deep red. From her slender body thick limbs protruded, seeming almost to rip out of her, or to grow like some sped-up tumor.

She fell from upright to sprawled-out and rose again on six insectoid legs. Mack wasn't there to see it or he would have said, "Oh, yeah, that's the firebolt-shooting thing from the causeway."

"It's called a Maradak, by the way," Risky said, her voice unsurprisingly slurred by the fact that her mouth was dribbling liquid fire. "And it eats only one thing. Liver."

There were cries of "Ewwww."

Then Risky added, "Human liver."

And then the terror started for real. There were screams and cries and fleeing. Mack's parents raced back to their car and sped off—without their popcorn!

"You're dying first," Risky said, glaring at Camaro. "I thought I already had you killed once."

"I'm not so easy to kill," Camaro said.

Camaro should have run. Any normal person

would have run. But Camaro was not one of those cowardly bullies; she was like Stefan: pretty darned brave, really.

So she put up her fists.

Risky put up her claws, teeth, bulging reptilian muscles, and eye protrusions that dripped fire and ice.

The Destroyer frowned.

Camaro knew she was about to die. She would need a miracle to get out of this jam.

The last miracle she'd seen was Mack moving the Eiffel Tower.

Risky roared, a sound that shook the earth and bruised the air.

And for some reason, in that moment of terror— yes, Camaro felt terror—the thing that came to mind was the last thing Mack had said in the last YouTube video.

"Fla-ma ik ag San Francisco!"

Twenty-five

Hurricanes are amazing things. Hurricanes can be killers, as can earthquakes. Neither is a joke, that's for sure.

And suddenly the San Francisco Bay Area was getting hit with both at once. Because as incredible as it may seem, the power of the Magnificent Eleven, armed with the words of Vargran and the *enlightened puissance*, could bring on a hurricane. And at the same time the terrible evil power of the Pale Queen, causing solid rock to heave itself up out of the sea to form a bridge, was making the earth shift and groan and shudder and shake.

People were hurt that day.

People were hurt. And that is a terrible, terrible thing. If you feel like crying for the people who were hurt, well, good. Because we should cry for people who are hurt.

But Mack couldn't stop the earthquake, and the hurricane was the only way he could think of to stop the attack of creatures who would have rampaged unchecked through the city and then the state and country and finally the world.

It was a necessary evil. But a necessary evil is still an evil.

The storm came on in a gray wall a thousand feet high. It made everything else seem small and weak and insignificant. It came on at 110 miles an hour.

"Hold on!" Mack cried.

"Grab the railing, get your heads down, and hold on!" Stefan cried, adding useful detail.

The storm did not touch the mile-long parade of fell creatures. They were protected by the Pale Queen's invisible force field. But the storm had an odd effect anyway, because the vacuum created by the onrushing wind sucked hundreds of them out of the open end of the barrier, like sucking them through a straw.

Lepercons, Tong Elves, Skirrit, Bowands, and even mighty Gudridan were sucked out and thrown up into the air, and flew like flailing, bellowing cannonballs at the Golden Gate Bridge.

A Bowand hit the vertical cable directly above Mack's head with such force that the creature was cut in two and both halves flew on.

Mack had a grip on the railing but the wind was so strong he felt his fingers slipping. Sylvie lost her grip and was rescued by a lightning-quick grab from Jarrah.

"This is insane!" José cried, and Mack only heard him because José was gripping the same two feet of railing.

Ilya's wheelchair brake was no match for the storm and his chair began to slide. Stefan, leaning hard into the wind, practically horizontal, with his shoes slipping, grabbed the wheelchair and kept it from getting away.

All the while the Pale Queen's creatures were battered against the support towers, the roadway, the railings, the cables. Many more were simply blown beneath the bridge to hit the water on the far side.

Then, in the midst of mayhem, the earth rolled. It was more than an earthquake. It was the earth as a heaving, bucking bull in a rodeo. The bridge shuddered and whipped. The entire roadway was like a writhing snake. Pieces of pavement broke loose, were snatched by the wind and hurled away. A car rolled over and slammed into the far side rail.

It was madness. It was death and destruction.

Mack raised his head and squeezed an eye open and saw that now even the Pale Queen's magic had weakened. The barrier that had protected her creatures was broken in places, and the monster army was sucked out of numerous holes, landing in the churning sea and drowning.

But the storm hurt good as well as evil. The police SWAT team was nowhere to be seen. The helicopters were crumpled wrecks. The Coast Guard ship was crunched against the northern bridge pier.

The wind began to die down. The earthquake's force lessened. Mack shot a frightened look toward the city. Most of the wind had blown straight through the

Golden Gate but had only struck a sideways blow at the city. Still, Mack could see broken windows in the tall buildings of downtown—broken windows and dead monsters sliding down the slanted face of the Transamerica Pyramid. Like bugs that had hit a car windshield, they had left smeary trails of guts.

The bridge still stood, but snapped cables hung down, and the road surface was a cracked, pitted mess. Dead or dying creatures stuck in the cables like grotesque parodies of birds sitting on power lines.

The Magnificent Eleven pulled themselves together. They twisted their windblown clothing back into place. They patted their hair down. They squished the flesh of their faces back into shape.

Down below, Mack saw that the Coast Guard ship had survived. It was bent in the middle, but it had survived. And the SWAT team and marines had managed to climb onto the vertical face of the stone pier before the winds hit. The wind had pinned them against it, and that had saved their lives.

But they looked shaken up. Well, everyone was shaken up.

"I think we did it," Rodrigo said.

"We shall see," Sylvie said doubtfully.

"O.M. GEEE!" Hillary said. "Is this what it's like hanging around with you people?"

Dietmar and Xiao were closest to Mack. They exchanged skeptical glances.

It was Stefan who said, "Better look at that."

They all followed the direction of Stefan's gaze. And they saw then that they had not won a victory, just a temporary reprieve.

The volcano had ceased to belch smoke and ash and lava. Now it was splitting open at the top, like a flower opening to the sun. It split in vast sections, like the sections of an orange.[44] The newly calmed sea rippled like someone shaking out a sheet to put on a bed. The sound of rock splitting and boulders rolling and dirt cascading came to their ears.

And from that volcano, from the underground world where she had been imprisoned for three thousand years, she rose.

The Pale Queen was come at last.

And all hope died.

---

44 You can go with flower or orange. Either works.

Twenty-six

The Pale Queen was like a fashionista in that she could wear anything. Anything at all. Only instead of a dress or a nice pair of slacks, she could do the same with her very body, her shape. The form she took.

Her powers were unlike anything the world had seen before.

A single hand rose from the volcano as the newly made, still steaming-hot mountain split apart. A single hand so big it was plainly visible from the bridge, miles away.

That hand had five fingers, each deathly white, each ending in a wickedly curved fingernail of some glittering metal. It might have been silver. It might have been titanium. It might have been some alloy forged in the deep bowels of the earth. One thing we know: those nails could sink into solid rock and rip it like a hunk of cheese.[45]

Behind that hand came an arm. An arm wreathed in a bracelet made of bones that seemed to have been dipped in that same silvery metal. The flesh of that arm was as pale as a sheet of paper, but more translucent. Within the flesh one could see the pumping arteries carrying blue blood, blood that would turn black if it were ever spilled.[46]

The arm rose like a tower, like a living skyscraper, straight up from that volcano and then! A second hand, a second arm, now squeezing out of the volcano.

A third! And it was too much for the mound of cooling, hissing lava. The volcano simply fell apart, rolled in massive chunks to splash into the sea.

And yet another arm, and then, something that was no arm.

---

45 I'm picturing cheddar.
46 Not much chance of that happening.

A head, with skin so white, so pale that the bone could be seen clearly, as if someone had taken a skull and stretched skin as sheer as a white stocking across it.

The hair atop that skull was long and brittle, as if it was not hair but flexible quills. The hair spilled out over the ruins of the volcano and hung in the sea, causing the water to boil.

Then . . . Then Mack saw, and his heart stopped. For at last her eyes . . . He was seeing the Pale Queen, seeing her eyes, her eyes . . . and she could see him!

The eyes were palest blue where they should have been white. The irises were like a snake's eyes, vertical slits of silver. The pupil was a black fire, a coal edged with red, and it widened in terrible joy as it focused on the eleven of them.

Mack could almost hear her thoughts.

Only eleven! the Pale Queen thought. Only eleven! Followed by a wicked laugh.

She rose, and the earth and sea split open to allow her. Higher and higher. Until six arms were clear, and a long insect-like body, white and streaked with yellow filth.

She was huge. She was vast. Dinosaurs could have been her lapdogs.

From out of the north two military jets came screaming toward her. They fired missiles.

The missiles exploded in midair. The jets exploded next.

More missiles, fired from jets unseen or from drones, and these, too, exploded, making insignificant red flowers in midair.

Now, she opened wide her mouth. And here at last could be seen indelible colors, for within that gaping maw, behind those tarantula teeth, were the very fires of hell.

There came a sound. But it was no single sound, it was layer upon layer of sound. It was made up of the screams of every poor, unlucky creature who had ever angered the Pale Queen.

It was the sound of agony. It was the sound of terror. It was the sound of madness and the death of joy and the end of the world.

The voice of the Pale Queen screamed, and for a thousand miles in every direction men and women and children heard it and knew that the end had come. They fell to their knees. They lost control of their bowels. They drove their cars off the road and dropped what they were holding and covered their ears in a desperate, pointless attempt to block that awful sound.

There were some—the old, the sick, the easily frightened—who died from that sound alone. Or at least wished they could.

Mack felt his insides turn to water. He, too, fell to his knees. The others, likewise, dropped, or fell on their backs, or curled up in a ball. The only one still upright was Ilya in his wheelchair.

I was a fool, Mack thought. I was a stupid little fool to think I could fight that!

At that moment he hated Grimluk for getting him into this. And he hated the *enlightened puissance*. He hated the whole world for conspiring somehow to put him here, now, against . . . against an evil so powerful that no one, no force, could possibly defeat her.

"Huh," Stefan said. "What are you doing here?"

Mack's lip was quivering, his throat was convulsing, his heart was hammering like it was trying to get the heck out of his chest, his arms were noodles, his legs were weak, but still, he was curious about what could possibly attract Stefan's attention away from the Pale Queen.

"I don't know what I'm doing here," a voice said. "But it looks like I have really bad timing."

A vaguely familiar voice.

Mack turned in disbelief. There could only be one explanation.

The final Magnifica.

Camaro Angianelli.

Twenty-seven

MEANWHILE, IN SEDONA

Risky stared at the place where the girl—
Mustang or Cabana or some such thing (Risky
had never been good with names)—had been seconds
before.

"Unh-garo!" the Destroyer cried.

It didn't take Risky long to figure out what had
happened. The girl—Camaro, yeah, that was her
name—had spoken the Vargran words that would
take her to Mack.

Was Camaro one of the Twelve? What would that give Mack? Had more joined him?

What if . . . Risky felt a thrill of fear. What if Camaro was the twelfth of the Twelve?

That would be a real good news–bad news situation for Risky. After all, she wanted her mother to be stopped and either killed outright or imprisoned for another few millennia or perhaps forever. And if Camaro was one of the Twelve, maybe even the twelfth, well, that would mean that at least in theory the Magnificent Twelve could defeat the Pale Queen.

In theory. It wouldn't be easy. Not at all a foregone conclusion.

On the other hand, if they could take down the Pale Queen, they could take Risky down as well.

So, in a perfect world the Twelve would succeed but manage to lose half their number. Then Risky would be able to manage them. In fact she might even be able to use them. It might be nice to have a few spare Magnifica around to handle the smaller evils that Risky would need to get done.

The worst thing would be if the Twelve prevailed against the Pale Queen and all of them survived.

Risky could not hope to deal with that. Not the twelve twelves.

Decision time. What to do?

"Destroyer!" Risky said.

"Yes."

"Did we not go over this? At the very least, *Yes, mistress*! Or *goddess*. Or *princess*. Your choice."

The Destroyer stared blankly at her.

"Interesting," Risky said under her breath. That was the problem. The Destroyer had no decision-making capability. She had noticed this before. If she gave him a choice, he'd be baffled. He would need very specific instructions.

"Minions!" Risky shrieked in a voice so big it had to be heard all across Sedona and up into the hills. It reached all the dark hidey-holes where the Skirrit and Tong Elves had hidden after the dance.

They came rushing from garages and sewers, from the closets of scared children and the reeking, indescribably filthy rooms of teenage boys. There was no great horde of them—her mother had allowed Risky to take only a handful of each, a dozen in all, but that was more than the tiny Sedona police force could deal with.

236

"Minions!" Risky cried. "I order you to heed my words. I order you to obey!"

"Yes, princess!"

"Yes, goddess!"

"Yes, mistress!" they cried, each making his own choice of preferred title. See, that was the problem, she thought, nodding. Well, live and learn.

"Okay, first things first," Risky shouted. "You will all address me as *goddess*!"

The Tong Elves and Skirrit were good with that. They'd always been confused on just what to call the Pale Queen's daughter and frankly they were happy to have the matter cleared up.

"Yes, goddess!" they cried with audible relief.

"You, too, Destroyer. You are to call me *goddess*!"

"Yes, goddess," the go— er, Destroyer said dutifully.

"Now, all of you listen to me! I want this town emptied out! I order you to terrorize these humans!

Make them quake and gibber and wet their pants with terror. And drive them from town! Drive them all away!"

"Hey!" one police officer protested, because this didn't sound like a nice thing to do.

"Drive them all from this place!" Risky cried, and raised her arms triumphantly in the air. "Drive them all away in terror! Ah-ha-ha-ha!"

And with that she disappeared, confident that when she returned there would not be a living soul left in Sedona, Arizona.

Just one little thing. Risky was not a native English speaker. She had overlooked the fact that English can be a very tricky language. A language full of homonyms.

Twenty-eight

"Camaro?"

"Mack?"

"You?"

"Here?"

"I had no idea."

"Me, neither."

"So, how's everything in Sedona?"

"Bad. Here?"

"Worse."

Mack waved his hand toward the volcano where

the world's greatest monster was literally ripping her way up out of the earth.

"Yeah, I noticed," Camaro said.

"Huh," Stefan said to Camaro.

"Yo," Camaro said back. They fist-bumped.

HHHUUUURRRGGGGAAAAAAWWWWW!

That last sound came from the Pale Queen. She was perfectly capable of speaking, but there was no one around to tell her to use her words.

She was a creature half insect, half human, eerily like the ant Mack had earlier had crawling across his eyeball, but with human hands and a mostly human-like head, and well, okay, there was nothing about the Pale Queen that was really familiar.

If nothing else, she existed on a scale that was simply impossible without great magic. The largest dinosaurs were cocker spaniels compared to her.

The air force and navy were fully awake now, and missiles—small ones, big ones—were zooming in from all directions, from jets overhead, from submarines far out in the ocean, and they would hit her with unerring accuracy and she didn't even notice. The pale plastic-like armor that covered her wasn't even stained by the explosions.

The naval destroyer that had come racing from the fleet far at sea was firing its deck guns and machine guns and missiles, and it may as well have been throwing spit wads.

In fact, at least people notice spit wads. The Pale Queen didn't even bother destroying the ship or the jets or the helicopters that swooped with crazy courage to fire machine guns straight at her face.

They were nothing to her.

They didn't even exist as far as she was concerned.

They could have all just slept in.

What the Pale Queen did notice was twelve kids standing on the Golden Gate Bridge.

Her terrible eyes were on them. Mack felt her gaze like a beam of fire and ice. He felt chilled to his core and shivered like you do when you have a really bad fever. Uncontrolled shivering.

But at the same time it felt as if his skin was burning. He had to look to convince himself it wasn't turning as crispy as rotisserie chicken.

Run, a voice in Mack's head said. Just run. Run far away.

He glanced left and right and saw fear in every eye. Well, except for Stefan. But all of them felt that fear, felt that temptation, felt that urge to turn and run away.

Fear is normal. Everyone has fear. (Okay, except Stefan.) Everyone wants to survive. Everyone wants evil to be someone else's problem. Don't they? Don't you? Don't I?

Most people live their lives and never have to come right up close with evil. Those people are lucky.

But some people can't escape it; some people are just standing there on a bridge when evil comes looking for them, and they could run. They could turn away and try to save themselves.

That's what most people do.

But fortunately for all of us, some people don't.

Some people stand their ground no matter how much their insides turn liquid and their muscles turn weak and their chests feel weighted down so they can hardly breathe.

We call those people brave.

On that day, at that time, facing an inconceivable evil and armed with only a few words and the strength inside them, the Magnificent Twelve did not run away.

The Pale Queen saw that resolve. And she felt fear, too.

Not that it stopped her. I mean, she'd been looking forward to this for three thousand years.

She began to move, and her speed was shocking. She was no ponderous, shuffling, slow-moving monster. Her six hands/legs churned the stone pier and the water on either side, and she moved!

"Hold hands," Mack ordered.

"What words?" Dietmar asked. For once he was letting Mack take the lead.

"We want this to end," Jarrah said. "We don't want someone else to deal with this in some distant future."

"End it," Sylvie agreed.

"*Stib-ma albi kandar,*" Xiao whispered. "Kill the Pale Queen."

The Pale Queen was a whole lot bigger than an express train and was moving as fast as one. She would hit them and snap the cables like threads and bring them all crashing down to their deaths.

"Everyone got that?" Mack asked.

"No problem," José said.

"This is so bogus," Hillary complained. But she repeated the words quietly to herself, ensuring she had them right.

"Five seconds," Stefan said.

"Yep," Mack said tersely.

Then he felt it. Like someone had hooked them all up to a power line. It was a vast and amazing thing. He had felt inklings of it before, but here, now, at last: they were the Magnificent Twelve, and the power that flowed through them and united them was like the power of exploding suns.

"Four," Stefan said

"Three."

"Two."

"Now!" Mack cried.

And with one voice, staring through tear-streaked eyes at the Pale Queen, focusing all their power on her, they shouted,

"Stib-ma albi kandar!"

Twenty-nine

At the last possible second the Pale Queen leaped. It was an astounding thing to see. She simply leaped over the Golden Gate Bridge. It was like a hundred 747s roaring just inches overhead.

The wind of her wake flattened the Magnificent Twelve.

"We missed!" Dietmar cried.

The Pale Queen plunged into the water of the bay, sending up a massive waterspout, swamping a container ship that had the bad luck to be in the wrong place at the wrong time.

For two long minutes she was hidden from view.

"Maybe we got her after all," Jarrah said.

But Mack didn't think so. And then they saw the water churn between Alcatraz and San Francisco's Fisherman's Wharf.

"She will attack the city," Dietmar said. "She's afraid of us so she attacks in a different direction."

And then, she began to rise from the water. Hand over hand, dragging her vast bulk up out of the sea. Heading straight into the heart of the city.

There she would kill and maim. She would crush and eat. She would destroy.

"We failed," Mack said. "We lose. The world loses. She wins. After all we've gone through. She wins."

"'When I despair, I remember that all through history the way of truth and love has always won. There have been tyrants and murderers, and for a time, they can seem invincible, but in the end, they always fall. Think of it—always.'" It was Ilya, the Russian boy in the wheelchair, who spoke.

Sylvie put a hand on his shoulder and looked at Mack. "Gandhi said that."

"Actually, it is a fake quote made up by a smart person who knew the internet would believe it was Gandhi," Dietmar said, "but it is an encouraging sentiment."

"Did the smart person ever meet the Pale Queen?" Jarrah asked sarcastically.

"She's attacking the city," Xiao said. "So help is on the way."

"What help?" Mack asked in despair. "She'll destroy the city in minutes. We can't even get there in time. What help is coming? Cops? The army?"

"More like the air force," Xiao said.

Mack looked at her and followed the direction of her gaze.

Buildings had risen from deep places beneath the city, from under the narrow, clogged streets of Chinatown. Buildings that had seemed dull and solid unfolded like pieces of origami, revealing an incredible network of underground halls and chambers.

The hidden realm of the dragons.

And now they rose slithering and sliding into the air. Dozens of them in all the colors of the rainbow. The dragons Mack had seen in China were huge, and so were these, but they were tiny compared to the Pale Queen.

"As you know, Mack, we have a treaty with the Western dragons," Xiao said. "Neither they nor we may fly freely in the other's territory. Unless one of our cities is threatened."

"One of your cities?"

"Beneath the streets of San Francisco are many amazing, unusual things you might never imagine," Xiao said.

"And quite a few right up on the streets of San Francisco," Valin said. Then shrugged. "I mean, that's what I hear."

"You went to them," Mack said to Xiao, recalling her brief absence earlier.

"They cannot fight the Pale Queen. But they can get us close to her," Xiao said.

"Are those flying snakes?" Camaro asked.

"So we get a second chance," Mack said.

The dragons reached the bridge just as the Pale Queen smashed three seafood restaurants and seven souvenir stands on Fisherman's Wharf.

The dragons swarmed around the bridge, looking

a little like giant, colorful kites.

The dragon in charge—an unusually multicolored, gilt-tipped, sneering-mouthed creature the size of a train—floated effortlessly in the air near the Magnifica.

"This is Jihao Long," Xiao said. "The name means, basically, Fabulous Dragon." She shrugged. "It's San Francisco."

"Where shall we take you?" Jihao Long asked.

"We're almost drained of *enlightened puissance*," Mack said. "We won't get a third try. This one has to be it. So we can't miss."

He looked at the others, and one by one they nodded. His decision. They would do whatever he decided. Even Valin. Even Dietmar.

"Put us right on top of her. Put us right on her head."

It took four dragons to carry them all. Xiao morphed back to her true self. Stefan lifted Ilya and his wheelchair as if they weighed nothing, and he and Jarrah and Ilya rode one of the great beasts.

Mack ended up with Dietmar and Sylvie, which was right, somehow. Annoying Dietmar and pretty, philosophical Sylvie.

They soared into the air and raced across the bay. Higher and higher until they could plainly see the Pale Queen. She was leaving a trail of devastation like nothing San Francisco had seen since the great earthquake of 1906, which pretty much destroyed the city.

The Pale Queen was done with Fisherman's Wharf and was on her way to the skyscrapers of downtown.

Intent on destruction, she did not look back toward the bridge. Or up at the sky. And she did not have eyes in the back of her head.

The dragons slowed and swooped down on her like fighter planes. They pulled up just above the top of her head, above what looked like a curved field of terrifyingly brittle hairs, each as thick as a telephone pole and ten times as long.

All together, the Magnificent Twelve jumped!

And at that exact moment the Pale Queen must have sensed something because she looked sharply up, and instead of falling toward a forest of hair, they were falling straight down toward that terrible eye.

It was the left eye—just so we have things straight here. The other eye was just as terrible.

"Ahhhhh!" Mack cried.

And the others made similar remarks.

They landed in a heap—actually two heaps—on the Pale Queen's cheek, just beneath her eye. And when Mack stood up, he was staring into an eye the size of a hot-air balloon.

The pupil, that black pit filled with cursed souls, rotated down, down, down to see them.

It adjusted, trying to find a focus point, obviously not quite sure what it was looking at.

"Grab hands!" Mack cried.

This time there was no surge of power. There was power, but oh, it was so much weaker. Too weak.

"Give it all you've got!" Mack shouted desperately. "For everyone you love! For the whole human race! Now!"

The pupil had focused.

It focused and then, suddenly, it widened out in sheer terror. Because she knew then what was happening. She knew who they were.

Desperately she swung her hand upward.

She roared in fury.

"Stib-ma albi kandar!"

A shudder, like another earthquake, went through her vast body. Mack could feel it.

"Don't let go!" Mack cried. "Give it all you've got!"

The Twelve held hands and focused with all their power, willing the Vargran spell to work.

A second shudder, more severe than the first. And this time the Pale Queen's roar carried a note of desperation.

Her hand swatted at them. It was like someone had dropped a building out of the sky, but they were shielded by being in a depression. Even so, the wind alone, and the kinetic force of the impact, knocked them down.

"Die!" Mack cried.

A third shudder . . . and when Mack looked up, he saw a light going out in that terrible eye.

The Pale Queen sagged downward.

And then, a terror none of them could have imagined. From her dimming pupil flew ghostly figures, wraiths. Most must have once been human, and they ranged from children to old men and women: the souls that the Pale Queen had taken over her long and awful life.

The wraiths flew like bats exiting a cave. And as

they emerged from the Pale Queen's shadow, they glittered in the sunlight and disappeared.

The Pale Queen fell forward like a giant tree and smashed her face into the Transamerica Pyramid. The impact tore all of the Magnifica loose. They flew through the air, spinning and screaming, and then smashed against the steep glass slope of the building.

The dragons raced to catch them. And they succeeded.

With supernatural speed, the dragons swept them up as they fell.

Until.

Standing atop an adjacent skyscraper stood a beautiful girl with piercing green eyes and flaming red hair.

From her outstretched hand came a jet of flame that passed inches from the eyes of Fabulous Dragon. He flinched and missed the final rescue.

And Dietmar fell.

He fell four hundred feet and smashed into a parked car.

Risky met Mack's horrified gaze and laughed.

"Eleven, now," Risky cried, and was gone. "Eleven!"

Thirty

The Pale Queen's body lay sprawled across down-town San Francisco. Her torso was mostly squeezed between the buildings on either side of Montgomery Street. Her arms stretched up Columbus and down Washington Street.

It was going to be one heck of a mess to clean up. Mack thought he and the others might come back in a few days, if they survived, and help with that.

But right now they still had work to do.

The mayor of San Francisco was there as Dietmar's

body was being taken away.

"You saved the city," the mayor said.

"We saved the world," Jarrah said pointedly.

"We didn't save Dietmar," Mack said grimly. Mack had never really liked Dietmar—which may be why he felt so guilty.

Dietmar was not the only one to die that day. Evil takes a toll. There's a price to be paid for freedom. It could have been much worse. They all knew it could have been much worse. But all Mack could think about now was Dietmar.

Camaro grabbed his shoulders. "Listen to me, Mack. This isn't over. She has plans."

"Who?"

"The redhead; who do you think? She's got the golem under her control. She thinks she's the new Pale Queen. She's not done yet, which means, neither are you!"

"But we're only eleven now," Mack said dully.

"No," Camaro said. "Eleven plus Stefan, plus all the bullies, plus—most important—the golem."

"But you said Risky has him under control."

"Yeah, well, I think something has changed with

the golem. I think maybe he's not so easy to control."

Mack shook his head. "You don't understand, Camaro. He's just a sort of mindless robot made out of mud and clay. He is whatever he's programmed to be."

Camaro looked fierce then. "And I say he's more than that. Anyway, you want to take down the red-head? She'll be with the golem: back in Sedona."

The mayor was still nearby, directing police and firefighters. The city was in a mess. There were surviving Tong Elves and Skirrit still running around the streets.

It was a very tough day in the life of the mayor, and he would have many, many more tough days ahead.

But he had not forgotten Mack, and when Mack tugged at his sleeve and said, "We need a favor," the mayor was quick to respond.

Phone calls were made, and thirty minutes later the Magnificent Twelve . . . Eleven . . . were on board a military jet racing toward Sedona.

Thirty-one

SEDONA

It's about 626 miles, give or take, from San Francisco to Sedona. The flight lasted about an hour and a half.

Sedona's airport is basically just a landing strip. It's not exactly JFK or O'Hare or one of those big, busy places.

The jet landed, and because it was an air force jet there was no Jetway, just a ramp, and they were let off on the hot tarmac under an Arizona sun.

Eleven twelve-year-olds with the *enlightened puissance*. Jarrah, Xiao, Sylvie, Charlie, Rodrigo, Valin, Ilya, Hillary, José, Camaro, and Mack.

And one fifteen-year-old.

They were not all friends. Some of them had only shown up hours before. Some, like Mack and Valin, had been enemies. But now they were all united by a common experience: they had all faced the Pale Queen.

And they had all seen Dietmar fall to his death.

And they knew who was responsible.

The mayor of San Francisco and the United States Air Force had arranged for a truck to meet them as they got off the plane. The truck drove them into Sedona.

"So, this is your home," Jarrah said. "Not so different from mine, really. Dry and hot."

"It was my home," Mack said. "I don't know if it still is."

He was changed, our Mack. And he felt it.

"Where to?" the driver asked.

Mack thought about it. "Back to where it all started. Richard Gere Middle School."[47]

"Richard Gere?" Hillary asked. "Seriously?"

---

47 Oooh, sorry, Fighting Pupfish.

Camaro shot the girl a dirty look. "Don't be dissing our school."

"It's Sedona," Mack said. "It was either Richard Gere or Lisa Simpson."

He nodded at Camaro and held out a fist. She bumped it. Stefan laid his big hand over theirs. It was a moment of Sedona solidarity.

Stefan said, "We take down the redhead."

"We do," Mack agreed.

"And the golem?" Camaro couldn't keep a tremulousness from her voice.

"It's not his fault," Mack said. "He's innocent. But so was Dietmar. And sometimes life is not fair."

Suddenly a dozen cars and a few pickup trucks went careening past heading away from the town. They were driven by Tong Elves and Skirrit. In each car were people. Men, women, and children. Many had their pets with them and some had tied bikes to the roof racks.

This mystery would puzzle Mack for some time until later investigations would turn up Risky's last furious order to her minions: drive the people out of town.[48]

---

48 Tricky language, English. Very tricky language.

The truck pulled to a stop and they climbed out. Mack gasped. The school was a pile of broken slabs of stucco and jagged wooden beams and shattered Spanish tile.

In all honesty, neither Mack nor Camaro nor Stefan was entirely distraught at the destruction. So long as no one was hurt, it was . . . Well, what kid hasn't fantasized about their school being destroyed?

But then Mack heard the sounds of destruction coming from downtown. Sedona's downtown was mostly just a single street, and in some ways it looked like an old-fashioned cowboy town. The buildings were not tall, nor were they cramped, nor were they all flashy with lots of lights. This was not New York or Los Angeles. Sedona was a small, squat western town overawed by bleak desertscape mountains. It was a place of cozy bed-and-breakfasts rather than big resort hotels. There were far more spiritual healers than there were stockbrokers, but there were also people with real businesses: restaurants, shops, dentist's offices, hardware stores—useful things.

Some of those useful things were now smoking ruins. An antiques-and-collectibles shop had been crushed beneath a FedEx truck. A tiny café that served all variations on avocado was burning. The cheese shop emitted a horrible smell—it alone was undamaged.

Down the street Mack saw the Destroyer. As Mack watched, the Destroyer snapped a light pole, then ripped one of those big metal mailboxes up off the ground and bit off the top as if he expected to find candy inside. Letters and cards scattered, caught by the breeze.

That was a federal crime.

It made Mack angry. He'd already seen San Francisco devastated. He did not want to see the same in his own hometown.

"Everyone with me," he commanded.

Yes: commanded. Because this was not the same old, diffident Mack. This was a Mack who had faced down the world's greatest evil. This was a Mack who had seen a friend fall to his death. He wasn't playing anymore. He was deadly serious.

The eleven, plus Stefan, began to march down the street toward the Destroyer, who carried on happily smashing things while still clutching the faded-blue steel mailbox.

"Destroyer!" Mack called when they were within range.

The Destroyer stopped.

Slowly he turned.

He no longer looked anything like Mack. He was ten feet tall, a monster of dead eyes and blank visage.

"Urrgh?" the Destroyer said.

"It's me, Golem. Or Destroyer. Whatever you are now. It's me, Mack MacAvoy. And I'm ordering you to stop."

The Destroyer stared at him. Probably. It's hard to tell where a blank-eyed creature is staring.

Then it began to advance on Mack.

"Get ready," Mack said to his friends. "We need a spell to destroy him."

"What?" Camaro cried. "What do you mean, destroy him? That's the golem!"

"We have no choice," Mack said.

"No. No, no, no," Camaro said. "No one is destroying the golem. That's what she wants you to do."

Mack knew who Camaro meant by "she."[49] It made him hesitate, but only for a moment. "It has to

---

49 Risky, duh.

be stopped. It has to be destroyed."

"It's not an it," Camaro pleaded. "It's a he. He is a real person underneath all that."

"No, he is just a golem," Valin argued.

Camaro got right in Valin's face. Valin wasn't scared easily. But he took a step back. A big step.

"You don't know him," Camaro raged. "I know him. I can get him to stop."

By this point the Destroyer was practically on them.

Mack nodded at Camaro. "You can try." To everyone else he said, "Hold hands and be ready."

"Golem," Camaro pleaded. "Listen to me. I know you're still in there some—"

With startling speed, the Destroyer lunged. With a single powerful hand he brought the torn mailbox up high, then brought it down with shocking suddenness.

Right on Mack.

Or more accurately, right around Mack. It was like someone slamming a glass down to trap a bug. Except that this glass was small compared to the "bug." The mailbox's bottom slammed down on Mack's head. He fell to his knees. His head swam and for a few moments he was completely unconscious.

The Destroyer scooped one big hand beneath the open part of the mailbox, lifted the whole thing in the air, and squeezed.

With a sound like a slow-motion car accident, the metal shards of the opening began to close. For the Destroyer it was like crushing aluminum foil. In seconds Mack was completely trapped, enclosed, inside a steel box.

The Destroyer tossed the metal prison aside. It landed hard and Mack cried out.

Stefan threw himself at the box, trying to pry it open, knowing what would happen.

Mack's consciousness came back on a wave of dread more awful than anything he had ever felt before. His hands battered at the steel cage. His eyes searched for light. His knees were pressed up against his chest, he could barely breathe, and the Arizona sun was already raising the temperature to more than a hundred degrees.

Mack had twenty-one known phobias. But the greatest of these, the master phobia, the one phobia that outdid all the others, was claustrophobia.

Claustrophobia. The fear of being locked in a small space, unable to get out, unable to breathe, unable . . .

Those outside heard a soul-wrenching wail. It was a sound that started as a cry but rose and rose and with each second became more panicky.

They heard Mack pounding, kicking, battering his hands and knees and feet to pulp trying to smash his way out.

"Don't panic, don't panic," Stefan cried as even his great strength failed to budge the steel.

A single car, a convertible, drove down the street, going at a leisurely pace. Taking its time. Just the one vehicle.

The top was down, and it was easy to see the red hair flowing in the breeze.

Risky was coming to claim her prize.

Thirty-two

STILL SEDONA

She stepped out wearing a lovely summer dress—gold and green (the green matched her eyes) and patterns in black (to match her heart).

"Well, isn't this a nice little get-together?" Risky said pleasantly.

Mack was screaming incoherently in the trap at her feet. The Destroyer loomed behind her, ready to do her bidding.

Stefan ran straight at her. Risky looked annoyed,

flicked her finger, and sent Stefan flying backward to crash beside Camaro Angianelli.

Risky knelt and with a puckish smile that showed off her excellent teeth tapped on the mailbox. "Is that you, Mack?"

Mack stopped screaming.

"It must be getting stuffy in there," Risky said. "Are you getting enough air?"

"You know he's not, you evil witch," Jarrah snapped.

"Oh, I know," Risky said, and her smile was feral now. "He's more frightened than he's ever been in his life. He can't control himself. He's like a mad beast in there."

"Let him go!" Sylvie demanded.

"Hmm. Short, aren't you?" Risky said, giving Sylvie the once-over. She stood all the way up, rested one foot on the mailbox, and said, "There are only ten of you now that Mack is . . . preoccupied. And ten of you don't have the power to defeat me. Especially not without your leader. No, without Mack you have less than half the power you have with him. Did you know that? He's the greatest of you. You're all just . . . accessories."

"I'll accessorize you!" Camaro yelled, and lashed out

at Risky with a kick. She actually managed to kick Risky in the knee.

"Ow! That hurt!" Risky yelled angrily. "Destroyer! Take her! Then . . . take her apart!"

The Destroyer moved swiftly to grab Camaro around the waist. Camaro didn't scream or struggle.

"Now, let's get down to business," Risky said. "It's hard work ruling the world. It's hard and lonely work. I think it's the loneliness that made my mother so cranky. Well, that plus the whole evil thing. But loneliness, too. I don't want to end up like her. I want a consort."

"A concert?" Charlie asked.

"A consort. Consort. A partner. A henchman. A partner in crime. A—"

"Boyfriend?" Xiao asked incredulously.

The Destroyer drew Camaro close. It tightened its grip around her waist, and Camaro let out an involuntary cry. She put her arms around the monster's neck and seemed to be trying to choke him back. Useless, of course: you can't choke a Destroyer. You just can't.

"Long ago I found someone," Risky said wistfully. "His name was Gil. He worshipped me, and I did not eat him or dismember him or set him on fire. No, we were close, me and Gil."

Risky sighed heavily. "But Mother scared him off. He was devastated by losing me. He went on to be a warrior and ended up starring in some epic, but the point is he never got over me. He loved me. I could see it in his eyes. Just as I can see it in Mack's eyes when he looks at me."

"You are insane," Sylvie said matter-of-factly as the Destroyer drew Camaro ever closer, probably preparing to bite her head off.

Risky sat on the mailbox and crossed her legs and looked very smug and in charge. "Join me, Mack. Swear true faith and allegiance to me, and I will set you free."

Mack was no longer screaming. But he was gasping for breath, panting and wheezing in abject terror.

"The next step is digging a hole and burying you," Risky said. She winked at the others as if this was a flirtatious little joke.

"Noooooooooo!" Mack cried.

"Join me, Mack," Risky crooned. "Join me."

"Noooooo. N-n-n-n-no. No. NO. I. WILL. NOT!"

Stefan had been readying another futile charge. He stopped dead in his tracks.

Stefan had been with Mack from the beginning. No one knew more about Mack's phobias. No one had seen more of Mack's meltdowns. No one except for Mack himself had a clearer understanding of the sheer terror Mack was suffering.

"Huh," Stefan said. And by that single word Stefan meant, "That is the bravest thing I've ever seen."

"What do you mean, no?" Risky demanded.

"NO! NO! NOOOOOO!" Mack roared.

And at that very moment, Camaro, squeezed and choking and feeling an awful lot like an overcooked sausage about to burst open, had her first kiss.

With all her strength she pushed her face toward the Destroyer and pressed her lips against his . . . well, they were lips of a sort.

Then she drew back, barely able to breathe, and whispered, "You are not the Destroyer. You are Golem. And I love you."

It's an interesting historical fact that the ancient rabbis who first created golems as powerful creatures meant to protect the weak (and of course kill enemies) had never attempted at any time to kiss a golem.

This was unprecedented in golem history.

Also, no one had ever loved a golem before. This is fact, this isn't something made up.

The golem's whole personality, character, mission is determined by the placement of a message in its mouth. No one had ever tried to put anything in a golem's heart.

"I love you," Camaro said. "The real you. So please don't kill me."

Risky heard none of this, of course, because she was busy raging at Mack. "I'll bury you alive! You diss me? Do you know who I am? I am the goddess Ereskigal, also known as Hel and a bunch of other names. I am the princess of darkness! I am evil made flesh! And I'm far more beautiful than that short French girl there!"

Sylvie could have been insulted but she was far too sophisticated to imagine that life is some farcical contest to see who can best exemplify a superficial aesthetic judgment, a judgment so often based on the needs of a capitalist marketing machine that must by its very nature . . . (This went on for quite a while longer in Sylvie's head.)

"How DARE you reject ME!" Risky roared, and it was a roar because suddenly she was transforming from a very attractive redhead to a gruesome beast of terrible shape, with a head like a bull and a—

And that's when the Destroyer punched her. It was just one punch in her bull head. But a Destroyer is very strong, and this particular Destroyer was really tired of Risky yelling at everyone, so that single blow sent her flying. She landed ten feet away, on her monster behind.

She shook her head, dazed, and resumed her usual look.

"Get Mack out of there!" Stefan yelled to the Destroyer, who was already losing his more Destroyerish features and looking more like the golem.

The Destroyer/golem easily ripped the box open, and out tumbled a sweaty, bruised, and very relieved Mack.

Also angry.

"Okay," Mack snarled. "That's it."

Without even being asked, the eleven joined hands. And the golem joined hands, too, because it liked to belong. And Stefan figured, well, why not? So he also joined hands.

They formed a semicircle around Risky, who was still not entirely recovered.

"Like we did to the Pale Queen," Mack said.

In all eleven minds the Vargran spell replayed.

"One . . . ," Xiao counted.

"Two . . . ," Jarrah said.

"Three!" Mack cried.

"No! A life for a life!" Risky shrieked. "Let me live. A life for a life!"

"What do you mean by this?" Xiao demanded sharply.

"You give me my life, I give you a life," Risky said quickly. "I am a goddess, after all. I can give you back a life. One-for-one trade. I live and . . ." She let it hang there.

"Dietmar?" Mack said. "Do you mean Dietmar?"

"If you mean Dirtmore, yes," Risky said.

"No," Mack said, not liking himself right then. "How many people will you kill? We can't let you loose on the world, Goddess Ereskigal. Not even for our friend's life."

"I . . ." She swallowed hard, and her perfect lips quivered. "If I . . ." It was something she could barely bring herself to say. "If I . . . I could . . ." She slumped, defeated. "I would give up my power. Renounce my nature and become . . . just a girl. Just the most beautiful girl in the world and much prettier than Shrimpy McFrench girl there."

"You can do that? You can bring Dietmar back and renounce your power?" Mack asked.

It turned out she could.

And she did.

Suddenly, there was Dietmar.

"Dude," Mack said. "You were dead."

"Surely not," Dietmar said dismissively. "Perhaps an illusion of death."

Mack instantly disliked him again, but he was still glad to see him alive. He turned to Risky. "Now the rest. You have to de-goddess yourself and become a regular girl."

Risky sighed deeply. "It's no fun being a goddess, anyway," she said. "Not if you won't worship me."

She held up her hands, palms out, then with a sad expression said, "At this time, in this squalid little town, before these inferiors, I hereby renounce my power, my godhood, my immortality, and my membership to the Valhalla spa. I will henceforth no longer be Ereskigal, princess of evil, and will instead be mortal. A regular girl."

She bowed her head and said, "Make it so."

And suddenly the sky was darkened by a noisy flight of ravens. And then came the swirl of bats.

And it was finally over.

Well, over except that the sun started spinning in

the sky before finally stabilizing.

Finally, the terrible saga had reached an end.

Except for a terrible moaning sound that rose from the very earth itself like a chorus of vengeful ghosts.

And that was it.

Except for a sudden, freezing wind that chilled them all, then blew away.

And thus it was done and over.

Except for the remaining popcorn on the hibachi all popping with a single, gigantic pop that made everyone jump.

And that was it.

No, really.

The End

I t didn't take long to build a new school. It's amazing how quickly construction goes when you have
the help of Vargran. When it was finished, it was chris-
tened Mack MacAvoy Middle School.[50]

And by then Mack was no longer twelve years old.
He had turned thirteen. The *enlightened puissance* still
flowed through him, but it was more sluggish than
before.

The Magnificent Twelve all went their separate ways: Valin to India, Jarrah to Australia,

---

50   Go, Fighting Magnifica!

Dietmar—who still refused to believe he had been dead—to Germany, Xiao to China, Ilya to Russia, Hillary to Canada, Rodrigo to Argentina, Charlie to Britain, José to Brazil.

Sylvie was the last to leave.

"I'll miss you," Mack said to her.

"But you will come to visit in the fall, when the school named after me is finished, yes?"

"I'll be there. You can count on me."

Sylvie smiled. "Nothing is certain in this world, Mack. Except for the certainty that I can count on you."

Then she was gone, and Stefan, who had said at least three "Huhs" expressing various emotions on seeing Jarrah off, joined Mack and Camaro and Camaro's boyfriend for a cheeseburger.

Camaro's boyfriend looked a little like Mack, but a little not, too. He had his own thing going on, his own style, his own look. A look that involved the occasional twig protruding from his neck. He called himself Mick, not Mack, and he was a renowned dancer.

Mack never heard from Grimluk again, though he often stood staring into bathroom mirrors and fixtures. (This was tolerated because Mack was, after all, the greatest hero on earth.)

"So," Mack said, biting into his cheeseburger, "I guess it's all over."

Stefan nodded glumly and took a cheeseburger from a kid at the next table. (Bully habits die hard.) But then he reluctantly handed it back and bit into his own. "Huh," he said. And added, "Huh," which in this case meant, "Look at that."

Mack turned, and three booths away sat a girl with red hair and green eyes. She was sitting with three other girls—cheerleaders from the newly renamed Stefan Marr High School.

Standing next to the booth were two boys from the varsity football team.

She had lots of friends.

Risky saw Mack looking at her. And winked. Mack shuddered.

Mack MacAvoy was not an unlikely hero. He was an impossible hero. After all, he suffered from twenty-one—no, twenty-two identified phobias.

The most recent of which was a morbid fear of red-heads.

A Note to Fans

The Magnificent Twelve would never have existed but for my editor and friend, Katherine Tegen.

And there wouldn't have been much point in writing these four books without you, the readers. I am convinced that you are the smartest, most perceptive readers in the world. I suspect each of you has at least a little of the *enlightened puissance*. Thanks for reading. I hope you had a laugh or two.

— Michael Grant